A Modern Cinderella;

Or, The Little Old Shoe,
and Other Stories

Louisa May Alcott

A Modern Cinderella; Or, The Little Old Shoe, and Other Stories

ISBN: 978-1-64799-500-3

CONTENTS

A MODERN CINDERELLA
OR
THE LITTLE OLD SHOE

HOW IT WAS LOST

Among green New England hills stood an ancient house, many-gabled, mossy-roofed, and quaintly built, but picturesque and pleasant to the eye; for a brook ran babbling through the orchard that encompassed it about, a garden-plat stretched upward to the whispering birches on the slope, and patriarchal elms stood sentinel upon the lawn, as they had stood almost a century ago, when the Revolution rolled that way and found them young.

One summer morning, when the air was full of country sounds, of mowers in the meadow, black-birds by the brook, and the low of kine upon the hill-side, the old house wore its cheeriest aspect, and a certain humble history began.

"Nan!"

"Yes, Di."

And a head, brown-locked, blue-eyed, soft-featured, looked in at the open door in answer to the call.

"Just bring me the third volume of 'Wilhelm Meister,' there's a dear. It's hardly worth while to rouse such a restless ghost as I, when I'm once fairly laid."

As she spoke, Di PUlled up her black braids, thumped the pillow of the couch where she was lying, and with eager eyes went down the last page of her book.

"Nan!"

"Yes, Laura," replied the girl, coming back with the third volume for the literary cormorant, who took it with a nod, still too content upon the "Confessions of a Fair Saint" to remember the failings of a certain plain sinner.

"Don't forget the Italian cream for dinner. I depend upon it; for it's the only thing fit for me this hot weather."

And Laura, the cool blonde, disposed the folds of her white gown more gracefully about her, and touched up the eyebrow of the Minerva she was drawing.

"Little daughter!"

"Yes, father."

"Let me have plenty of clean collars in my bag, for I must go at once; and some of you bring me a glass of cider in about an hour;— I shall be in the lower garden."

The old man went away into his imaginary paradise, and Nan into that domestic purgatory on a summer day,—the kitchen. There were vines about the windows, sunshine on the floor, and order everywhere; but it was haunted by a cooking-stove, that family altar whence such varied incense rises to appease the appetite of household gods, before which such dire incantations are pronounced to ease the wrath and woe of the priestess of the fire, and about which often linger saddest memories of wasted temper, time, and toil.

Nan was tired, having risen with the birds,—hurried, having many cares those happy little housewives never know,—and disappointed in a hope that hourly "dwindled, peaked, and pined." She was too young to make the anxious lines upon her forehead seem at home there, too patient to be burdened with the labor others should have shared, too light of heart to be pent up when earth and sky were keeping a blithe holiday. But she was one of that meek sisterhood who, thinking humbly of themselves, believe they are honored by being spent in the service of less conscientious souls, whose careless thanks seem quite reward enough.

To and fro she went, silent and diligent, giving the grace of willingness to every humble or distasteful task the day had brought her; but some malignant sprite seemed to have taken possession of her kingdom, for rebellion broke out everywhere. The kettles would boil over most obstreperously,—the mutton refused to cook with the meek alacrity to be expected from the nature of a sheep,—the stove, with unnecessary warmth of temper, would glow like a fiery furnace,—the irons would scorch,—the linens would dry,—and spirits would fail, though patience never.

Nan tugged on, growing hotter and wearier, more hurried and more hopeless, till at last the crisis came; for in one fell moment she tore her gown, burnt her hand, and smutched the collar she was preparing to finish in the most unexceptionable style. Then, if she had been a nervous woman, she would have scolded; being a gentle girl, she only "lifted up her voice and wept."

"Behold, she watereth her linen with salt tears, and bewaileth herself because of much tribulation. But, lo! Help cometh from afar: a strong man bringeth lettuce wherewith to stay her, plucketh berries to comfort her withal, and clasheth cymbals that she may dance for joy."

3

The voice came from the porch, and, with her hope fulfilled, Nan looked up to greet John Lord, the house-friend, who stood there with a basket on his arm; and as she saw his honest eyes, kind lips, and helpful hands, the girl thought this plain young man the comeliest, most welcome sight she had beheld that day.

"How good of you, to come through all this heat, and not to laugh at my despair!" she said, looking up like a grateful child, as she led him in.

"I only obeyed orders, Nan; for a certain dear old lady had a motherly presentiment that you had got into a domestic whirlpool, and sent me as a sort of life-preserver. So I took the basket of consolation, and came to fold my feet upon the carpet of contentment in the tent of friendship."

As he spoke, John gave his own gift in his mother's name, and bestowed himself in the wide window-seat, where morning-glories nodded at him, and the old butternut sent pleasant shadows dancing to and fro.

His advent, like that of Orpheus in hades, seemed to soothe all unpropitious powers with a sudden spell. The Fire began to slacken, the kettles began to lull, the meat began to cook, the irons began to cool, the clothes began to behave, the spirits began to rise, and the collar was finished off with most triumphant success. John watched the change, and, though a lord of creation, abased himself to take compassion on the weaker vessel, and was seized with a great desire to lighten the homely tasks that tried her strength of body and soul. He took a comprehensive glance about the room; then, extracting a dish from he closet, proceeded to imbrue his hands in the strawberries' blood.

4

"Oh, John, you needn't do that; I shall have time when I've turned the meat, made the pudding and done these things. See, I'm getting on finely now:—you're a judge of such matters; isn't that nice?"

As she spoke, Nan offered the polished absurdity for inspection with innocent pride.

"Oh that I were a collar, to sit upon that hand!" sighed John,—adding, argumentatively,

"As to the berry question, I might answer it with a gem from Dr. Watts, relative to 'Satan' and idle hands,' but will merely say, that, as a matter of public safety, you'd better leave me alone; for such is the destructiveness of my nature, that I shall certainly eat something hurtful, break something valuable, or sit upon something crushable, unless you let me concentrate my energies by knocking on these young fellows' hats, and preparing them for their doom."

Looking at the matter in a charitable light, Nan consented, and went cheerfully on with her work, wondering how she could have thought ironing an infliction, and been so ungrateful for the blessings of her lot.

"Where's Sally?" asked John, looking vainly for the functionary who usually pervaded that region like a domestic police-woman, a terror to cats, dogs, and men.

"She has gone to her cousin's funeral, and won't be back till Monday. There seems to be a great fatality among her relations; for one dies, or comes to grief in some way, about once a month. But I don't blame poor Sally for wanting to get away from this place now and then. I think I could find it in my heart to murder an imaginary friend or two, if I had to stay here long."

5

And Nan laughed so blithely, it was a pleasure to hear her.

"Where's Di?" asked John, seized with a most unmasculine curiosity all at once.

"She is in Germany with 'Wilhelm Meister'; but, though 'lost to sight, to memory clear'; for I was just thinking, as I did her things, how clever she is to like all kinds of books that I don't understand at all, and to write things that make me cry with pride and delight. Yes, she's a talented dear, though she hardly knows a needle from a crowbar, and will make herself one great blot some of these days, when the 'divine afflatus' descends upon her, I'm afraid."

And Nan rubbed away with sisterly zeal at Di's forlorn hose and inky pocket-handkerchiefs.

"Where is Laura?" proceeded the inquisitor.

"Well, I might say that she was in Italy; for she is copying some fine thing of Raphael's or Michael Angelo's, or some great creatures or other; and she looks so picturesque in her pretty gown, sitting before her easel, that it's really a sight to behold, and I've peeped two or three times to see how she gets on."

And Nan bestirred herself to prepare the dish Wherewith her picturesque sister desired to prolong her artistic existence.

"Where is your father?" John asked again, checking off each answer with a nod and a little frown.

"He is down in the garden, deep in some plan about melons, the beginning of which seems to consist in stamping the first proposition in Euclid all over the bed, and then poking a few seeds into the middle of each. Why, bless the dear man! I forgot it was time for the cider. Wouldn't you like to take it to him, John? He'd

6

love to consult you; and the lane is so cool, it does one's heart good to look at it."

John glanced from the steamy kitchen to the shadowy path, and answered with a sudden assumption of immense industry, —

"I couldn't possibly go, Nan, — I've so much on my hands. You'll have to do it yourself. 'Mr. Robert of Lincoln' has something for your private ear; and the lane is so cool, it will do one's heart good to see you in it. Give my regards to your father, and, in the words of 'Little Mabel's' mother, with slight variation, —

> 'Tell the dear old body
> This day I cannot run,
> For the pots are boiling over
> And the mutton isn't done.'"

"I will; but please, John, go in to the girls and be comfortable; for I don't like to leave you here," said Nan.

"You insinuate that I should pick at the pudding or invade the cream, do you? Ungrateful girl, leave me!" And, with melodramatic sternness, John extinguished her in his broad-brimmed hat, and offered the glass like a poisoned goblet.

Nan took it, and went smiling away. But the lane might have been the Desert of Sahara, for all she knew of it; and she would have passed her father as unconcernedly as if he had been an apple-tree, had he not called out, —

"Stand and deliver, little woman!"

She obeyed the venerable highwayman, and followed him to and fro, listening to his plans and directions with a mute attention that quite won his heart.

7

"That hop-pole is really an ornament now, Nan; this sage-bed needs weeding,—that's good work for you girls; and, now I think of it, you'd better water the lettuce in the cool of the evening, after I'm gone."

To all of which remarks Nan gave her assent; the hop-pole took the likeness of a tall figure she had seen in the porch, the sage-bed, curiously enough, suggested a strawberry ditto, the lettuce vividly reminded her of certain vegetable productions a basket had brought, and the bobolink only sung in his cheeriest voice, "Go home, go home! he is there!"

She found John—he having made a free-mason of himself, by assuming her little apron—meditating over the partially spread table, lost in amaze at its desolate appearance; one half its proper paraphernalia having been forgotten, and the other half put on awry. Nan laughed till the tears ran over her cheeks, and John was gratified at the efficacy of his treatment; for her face had brought a whole harvest of sunshine from the garden, and all her cares seemed to have been lost in the windings of the lane.

"Nan, are you in hysterics?" cried Di, appearing, book in hand. "John, you absurd man, what are you doing?"

"I'm helpin' the maid of all work, please marm." And John dropped a curtsy with his limited apron.

Di looked ruffled, for the merry words were a covert reproach; and with her usual energy of manner and freedom of speech she tossed "Wilhelm" out of the window, exclaiming, irefully.—

"That's always the way; I'm never where I ought to be, and never think of anything till it's too late; but it's all Goethe's fault. What does he write books full of smart 'Phillinas' and interesting

8

'Meisters' for? How can I be expected to remember that Sally's away, and people must eat, when I'm hearing the 'Harper' and little 'Mignon?' John, how dare you come here and do my work, instead of shaking me and telling me to do it myself? Take that toasted child away, and fan her like a Chinese mandarin, while I dish up this dreadful dinner."

John and Nan fled like chaff before the wind, while Di, full of remorseful zeal, charged at the kettles, and wrenched off the potatoes' jackets, as if she were revengefully pulling her own hair. Laura had a vague intention of going to assist; but, getting lost among the lights and shadows of Minerva's helmet, forgot to appear till dinner had been evoked from chaos and peace was restored.

At three o'clock, Di performed the coronation ceremony with her father's best hat; Laura retied his old-fashioned neckcloth, and arranged his white locks with an eye to saintly effect; Nan appeared with a beautifully written sermon, and suspicious ink-stains on the fingers that slipped it into his pocket; John attached himself to the bag; and the patriarch was escorted to the door of his tent with the triumphal procession which usually attended his out-goings and in-comings. Having kissed the female portion of his tribe, he ascended the venerable chariot, which received him with audible lamentation, as its rheumatic joints swayed to and fro.

"Good-bye, my dears! I shall be back early on Monday morning; so take care of yourselves, and be sure you all go and hear Mr. Emerboy preach to-morrow. My regards to your mother. John. Come, Solon!"

But Solon merely cocked one ear, and remained a fixed fact; for long experience had induced the philosophic beast to take for his

9

motto the Yankee maxim, "Be sure you're right, then go ahead! He knew things were not right; therefore he did not go ahead.

"Oh, by the way, girls, don't forget to pay Tommy Mullein for bringing up the cow: he expects it to-night. And Di, don't sit up till daylight, nor let Laura stay out in the dew. Now, I believe I'm off. Come, Solon!"

But Solon only cocked the other ear, gently agitated his mortified tail, as premonitory symptoms of departure, and never stirred a hoof, being well aware that it always took three "comes" to make a "go."

"Bless me! I've forgotten my spectacles. They are probably shut up in that volume of Herbert on my table. Very awkward to find myself without them ten miles away. Thank you, John. Don't neglect to water the lettuce, Nan, and don't overwork yourself, my little 'Martha.' Come—"

At this juncture Solon suddenly went off, like "Mrs. Gamp," in a sort of walking swoon, apparently deaf and blind to all mundane matters, except the refreshments awaiting him ten miles away; and the benign old pastor disappeared, humming "Hebron" to the creaking accompaniment of the bulgy chaise.

Laura retired to take her siesta; Nan made a small carbonaro of herself by sharpening her sister's crayons, and Di, as a sort of penance for past sins, tried her patience over a piece of knitting, in which she soon originated a somewhat remarkable pattern, by dropping every third stitch, and seaming ad libitum. If John bad been a gentlemanly creature, with refined tastes, he would have elevated his feet and made a nuisance of himself by indulging in a "weed;" but being only an uncultivated youth, with a rustic regard

10

for pure air and womankind in general, he kept his head uppermost, and talked like a man, instead of smoking like a chimney.

"It will probably be six months before I sit here again, tangling your threads and maltreating your needles, Nan. How glad you must feel to hear it!" he said, looking up from a thoughtful examination of the hard-working little citizens of the Industrial Community settled in Nan's work-basket.

"No, I'm very sorry; for I like to see you coming and going as you used to, years ago, and I miss you very much when you are gone, John," answered truthful Nan, whittling away in a sadly wasteful manner, as her thoughts flew back to the happy times when a little lad rode a little lass in a big wheelbarrow, and never spilt his load, — when two brown heads bobbed daily side by side to school, and the favorite play was "Babes in the Wood," with Di for a somewhat peckish robin to cover the small martyrs with any vegetable substance that lay at hand. Nan sighed, as she thought of these things, and John regarded the battered thimble on his finger-tip with increased benignity of aspect as he heard the sound.

"When are you going to make your fortune, John, and get out of that disagreeable hardware concern?" demanded Di, pausing after an exciting "round," and looking almost as much exhausted as if it had been a veritable pugilistic encounter.

"I intend to make it by plunging still deeper into 'that disagreeable hardware concern;' for, next year, if the world keeps rolling, and John Lord is alive, he will become a partner, and then—and then—"

The color sprang up into the young man's cheek, his eyes looked out with a sudden shine, and his hand seemed involuntarily to close, as if he saw and seized some invisible delight.

11

"What will happen then, John?" asked Nan, with a wondering glance.

"I'll tell you in a year, Nan, wait till then." and John's strong hand unclosed, as if the desired good were not to be his yet.

Di looked at him, with a knitting-needle stuck into her hair, saying, like a sarcastic unicorn, —

"I really thought you had a soul above pots and kettles, but I see you haven't; and I beg your pardon for the injustice I have done you."

Not a whit disturbed, John smiled, as if at some mighty pleasant fancy of his own, as he replied, —

"Thank you, Di; and as a further proof of the utter depravity of my nature, let me tell you that I have the greatest possible respect for those articles of ironmongery. Some of the happiest hours of my life have been spent in their society; some of my pleasantest associations are connected with them; some of my best lessons have come to me among them; and when my fortune is made, I intend to show my gratitude by taking three flat-irons rampant for my coat of arms."

Nan laughed merrily, as she looked at the burns on her hand; but Di elevated the most prominent feature of her brown countenance, and sighed despondingly, —

"Dear, dear, what a disappointing world this is! I no sooner build a nice castle in Spain, and settle a smart young knight therein, than down it comes about my ears; and the ungrateful youth, who might fight dragons, if he chose, insists on quenching his energies in a saucepan, and making a Saint Lawrence of himself by wasting his

12

life on a series of gridirons. Ah, if I were only a man, I would do something better than that, and prove that heroes are not all dead yet. But, instead of that, I'm only a woman, and must sit rasping my temper with absurdities like this." And Di wrestled with her knitting as if it were Fate, and she were paying off the grudge she owed it.

John leaned toward her, saying, with a look that made his plain face handsome, —

"Di, my father began the world as I begin it, and left it the richer for the useful years he spent here, — as I hope I may leave it some half-century hence. His memory makes that dingy shop a pleasant place to me; for there he made an honest name, led an honest life and bequeathed to me his reverence for honest work. That is a sort of hardware, Di, that no rust can corrupt, and which will always prove a better fortune than any your knights can achieve with sword and shield. I think I am not quite a clod, or quite without some aspirations above money-getting; for I sincerely desire that courage that makes daily life heroic by self-denial and cheerfulness of heart; I am eager to conquer my own rebellious nature, and earn the confidence of innocent and upright souls; I have a great ambition to become as good a man and leave as good a memory behind me as old John Lord."

Di winked violently, and seamed five times in perfect silence; but quiet Nan had the gift of knowing when to speak, and by a timely word saved her sister from a thunder-shower and her stocking from destruction.

"John, have you seen Philip since you wrote about your last meeting with him?"

The question was for John, but the soothing tone was for Di, who gratefully accepted it, and perked up again with speed.

"Yes; and I meant to have told you about it," answered John, plunging into the subject at once.

"I saw him a few days before I came home, and found him more disconsolate than ever,—' just ready to go to the Devil,' as he forcibly expressed himself. I consoled the poor lad as well as I could, telling him his wisest plan was to defer his proposed expedition, and go on as steadily as he had begun,—thereby proving the injustice of your father's prediction concerning his want of perseverance, and the sincerity of his affection. I told him the change in Laura's health and spirits was silently working in his favor, and that a few more months of persistent endeavor would conquer your father's prejudice against him, and make him a stronger man for the trial and the pain. I read him bits about Laura from your own and Di's letters, and he went away at last as patient as Jacob ready to serve another 'seven years' for his beloved Rachel."

"God bless you for it, John!" cried a fervent voice; and, looking up, they saw the cold, listless Laura transformed into a tender girl, all aglow with love and longing, as she dropped her mask, and showed a living countenance eloquent with the first passion and softened by the first grief of her life.

John rose involuntarily in the presence of an innocent nature whose sorrow needed no interpreter to him. The girl read sympathy in his brotherly regard, and found comfort in the friendly voice that asked, half playfully, half seriously,—

"Shall I tell him that he is not forgotten, even for an Apollo? that

14

Laura the artist has not conquered Laura the woman? and predict that the good daughter will yet prove the happy wife?"

With a gesture full of energy, Laura tore her Minerva from top to bottom, while two great tears rolled down the cheeks grown wan with hope deferred.

"Tell him I believe all things, hope all things, and that I never can forget."

Nan went to her and held her fast, leaving the prints of two loving but grimy hands upon her shoulders; Di looked on approvingly, for, though stony-hearted regarding the cause, she fully appreciated the effect; and John, turning to the window, received the commendations of a robin swaying on an elm-bough with sunshine on its ruddy breast.

The clock struck five, and John declared that he must go; for, being an old-fashioned soul, he fancied that his mother had a better right to his last hour than any younger woman in the land,—always remembering that "she was a widow, and he her only son."

Nan ran away to wash her hands, and came back with the appearance of one who had washed her face also: and so she had; but there was a difference in the water.

"Play I'm your father, girls, and remember that it will be six months before 'that John' will trouble you again."

With which preface the young man kissed his former playfellows as heartily as the boy had been wont to do, when stern parents banished him to distant schools, and three little maids bemoaned his fate. But times were changed now; for Di grew alarmingly rigid during the ceremony; Laura received the salute like a graceful

15

queen; and Nan returned it with heart and eyes and tender lips, making such an improvement on the childish fashion of the thing that John was moved to support his paternal character by softly echoing her father's words, — "Take care of yourself, my little 'Martha.'"

Then they all streamed after him along the garden-path, with the endless messages and warnings girls are so prone to give; and the young man, with a great softness at his heart, went away, as many another John has gone, feeling better for the companionship of innocent maidenhood, and stronger to wrestle with temptation, to wait and hope and work.

"Let's throw a shoe after him for luck, as dear old 'Mrs. Gummage' did after 'David' and the 'willin' Barkis!' Quick, Nan! you always have old shoes on; toss one, and shout, 'Good luck!'" cried Di, with one of her eccentric inspirations.

Nan tore off her shoe, and threw it far along the dusty road, with a sudden longing to become that auspicious article of apparel, that the omen might not fail.

Looking backward from the hill-top, John answered the meek shout cheerily, and took in the group with a lingering glance: Laura in the shadow of the elms, Di perched on the fence, and Nan leaning far over the gate with her hand above her eyes and the sunshine touching her brown hair with gold. He waved his hat and turned away; but the music seemed to die out of the blackbird's song, and in all the summer landscape his eyes saw nothing but the little figure at the gate.

"Bless and save us! here's a flock of people coming; my hair is in a toss, and Nan's without her shoe; run! fly, girls! or the Philistines will be upon us!" cried Di, tumbling off her perch in sudden alarm.

16

Three agitated young ladies, with flying draperies and countenances of mingled mirth and dismay, might have been seen precipitating themselves into a respectable mansion with unbecoming haste; but the squirrels were the only witnesses of this "vision of sudden flight," and, being used to ground-and-lofty tumbling, didn't mind it.

When the pedestrians passed, the door was decorously closed, and no one visible but a young man, who snatched something out of the road, and marched away again, whistling with more vigor of tone than accuracy of tune, "Only that, and nothing more."

HOW IT WAS FOUND

Summer ripened into autumn, and something fairer than

> "Sweet-peas and mignonette
> In Annie's garden grew."

Her nature was the counterpart of the hill-side grove, where as a child she had read her fairy tales, and now as a woman turned the first pages of a more wondrous legend still. Lifted above the many-gabled roof, yet not cut off from the echo of human speech, the little grove seemed a green sanctuary, fringed about with violets, and full of summer melody and bloom. Gentle creatures haunted it, and there was none to make afraid; wood-pigeons cooed and crickets chirped their shrill roundelays, anemones and lady-ferns looked up from the moss that kissed the wanderer's feet. Warm airs were all afloat, full of vernal odors for the grateful sense, silvery birches shimmered like spirits of the wood, larches gave their green tassels to the wind, and pines made airy music sweet and solemn, as they stood looking heavenward through veils of summer sunshine or shrouds of wintry snow.

Nan never felt alone now in this charmed wood; for when she came into its precincts, once so full of solitude, all things seemed to wear one shape, familiar eyes looked at her from the violets in the grass, familiar words sounded in the whisper of the leaves, grew conscious that an unseen influence filled the air with new delights, and touched earth and sky with a beauty never seen before. Slowly these Mayflowers budded in her maiden heart, rosily they bloomed and silently they waited till some lover of such lowly herbs should catch their fresh aroma, should brush away the fallen leaves, and lift them to the sun.

Though the eldest of the three, she had long been overtopped by the more aspiring maids. But though she meekly yielded the reins of government, whenever they chose to drive, they were soon restored to her again; for Di fell into literature, and Laura into love. Thus engrossed, these two forgot many duties which even bluestockings and inamoratos are expected to perform, and slowly all the homely humdrum cares that housewives know became Nan's daily life, and she accepted it without a thought of discontent. Noiseless and cheerful as the sunshine, she went to and fro, doing the tasks that mothers do, but without a mother's sweet reward, holding fast the numberless slight threads that bind a household tenderly together, and making each day a beautiful success.

Di, being tired of running, riding, climbing, and boating, decided at last to let her body rest and put her equally active mind through what classical collegians term "a course of sprouts." Having undertaken to read and know everything, she devoted herself to the task with great energy, going from Sue to Swedenborg with perfect impartiality, and having different authors as children have sundry distempers, being fractious while they lasted, but all the better for them when once over. Carlyle appeared like scarlet-fever, and raged violently for a time; for, being anything but a "passive bucket," Di became prophetic with Mahomet, belligerent with Cromwell, and made the French Revolution a veritable Reign of Terror to her family. Goethe and Schiller alternated like fever and ague; Mephistopheles became her hero, Joan of Arc her model, and she turned her black eyes red over Egmont and Wallenstein. A mild attack of Emerson followed, during which she was lost in a fog, and her sisters rejoiced inwardly when she emerged informing them that

> "The Sphinx was drowsy,
> Her wings were furled."

Poor Di was floundering slowly to her proper place; but she splashed up a good deal of foam by getting out of her depth, and rather exhausted herself by trying to drink the ocean dry.

Laura, after the "midsummer night's dream" that often comes to girls of seventeen, woke up to find that youth and love were no match for age and common sense. Philip had been flying about the world like a thistle-down for five-and-twenty years, generous-hearted, frank, and kind, but with never an idea of the serious side of life in his handsome head. Great, therefore, were the wrath and dismay of the enamored thistle-down, when the father of his love mildly objected to seeing her begin the world in a balloon with a very tender but very inexperienced aeronaut for a guide.

"Laura is too young to 'play house' yet, and you are too unstable to assume the part of lord and master, Philip. Go and prove that you have prudence, patience, energy, and enterprise, and I will give you my girl,—but not before. I must seem cruel, that I may be truly kind; believe this, and let a little pain lead you to great happiness, or show you where you would have made a bitter blunder."

The lovers listened, owned the truth of the old man's words, bewailed their fate, and yielded,—Laura for love of her father, Philip for love of her. He went away to build a firm foundation for his castle in the air, and Laura retired into an invisible convent, where she cast off the world, and regarded her sympathizing sisters through a grate of superior knowledge and unsharable grief. Like a devout nun, she worshipped "St. Philip," and firmly believed in his miraculous powers. She fancied that her woes set her apart from common cares, and slowly fell into a dreamy state, professing no interest in any mundane matter, but the art that first attracted Philip. Crayons, bread-crusts, and gray paper became glorified in Laura's eyes; and her one pleasure was to sit pale and still before her easel, day after day, filling her portfolios with the faces he had once admired. Her sisters observed that every Bacchus, Piping Faun, or Dying Gladiator bore some likeness to a comely countenance that heathen god or hero never owned; and seeing this, they privately rejoiced that she had found such solace for her grief.

Mrs. Lord's keen eye had read a certain newly written page in her son's heart,—his first chapter of that romance, begun in paradise, whose interest never flags, whose beauty never fades, whose end can never come till Love lies dead. With womanly skill she divined the secret, with motherly discretion she counselled patience, and her son accepted her advice, feeling that, like many a healthful herb, its worth lay in its bitterness.

"Love like a man, John, not like a boy, and learn to know yourself before you take a woman's happiness into your keeping. You and Nan have known each other all your lives; yet, till this last visit, you never thought you loved her more than any other childish friend. It is too soon to say the words so often spoken hastily,—so hard to be recalled. Go back to your work, dear, for another year; think of Nan in the light of this new hope: compare her with comelier, gayer girls; and by absence prove the truth of your belief. Then, if distance only makes her dearer, if time only strengthens your affection, and no doubt of your own worthiness disturbs you, come back and offer her what any woman should be glad to take,—my boy's true heart."

John smiled at the motherly pride of her words, but answered with a wistful look.

"It seems very long to wait, mother. If I could just ask her for a word of hope, I could be very patient then."

"Ah, my dear, better bear one year of impatience now than a lifetime of regret hereafter. Nan is happy; why disturb her by a word which will bring the tender cares and troubles that come soon enough to such conscientious creatures as herself? If she loves you, time will prove it; therefore, let the new affection spring and ripen as your early friendship has done, and it will be all the stronger for a summer's growth. Philip was rash, and has to bear his trial now, and Laura shares it with him. Be more generous, John; make your trial, bear your doubts alone, and give Nan the happiness without the pain. Promise me this, dear,—promise me to hope and wait."

The young man's eye kindled, and in his heart there rose a better chivalry, a truer valor, than any Di's knights had ever known.

21

"I'll try, mother," was all he said; but she was satisfied, for John seldom tried in vain.

"Oh, girls, how splendid you are! It does my heart good to see my handsome sisters in their best array," cried Nan, one mild October night, as she put the last touches to certain airy raiment fashioned by her own skilful hands, and then fell back to survey the grand effect.

"Di and Laura were preparing to assist at an event of the season," and Nan, with her own locks fallen on her shoulders, for want of sundry combs promoted to her sisters' heads and her dress in unwonted disorder, for lack of the many pins extracted in exciting crises of the toilet, hovered like an affectionate bee about two very full-blown flowers.

"Laura looks like a cool Undine, with the ivy-wreaths in her shining hair; and Di has illuminated herself to such an extent with those scarlet leaves that I don't know what great creature she resembles most," said Nan, beaming with sisterly admiration.

"Like Juno, Zenobia, and Cleopatra simmered into one, with a touch of Xantippe by way of spice. But, to my eye, the finest woman of the three is the dishevelled young person embracing the bed-post: for she stays at home herself, and gives her time and taste to making homely people fine,—which is a waste of good material, and an imposition on the public."

As Di spoke, both the fashion-plates looked affectionately at the gray-gowned figure; but, being works of art, they were obliged to nip their feelings in the bud, and reserve their caresses till they returned to common life.

"Put on your bonnet, and we'll leave you at Mrs. Lord's on our way.

It will do you good, Nan; and perhaps there may be news from John," added Di, as she bore down upon the door like a man-of-war under full sail.

"Or from Philip," sighed Laura, with a wistful look.

Whereupon Nan persuaded herself that her strong inclination to sit down was owing to want of exercise, and the heaviness of her eyelids a freak of imagination; so, speedily smoothing her ruffled plumage, she ran down to tell her father of the new arrangement.

"Go, my dear, by all means. I shall be writing; and you will be lonely if you stay. But I must see my girls; for I caught glimpses of certain surprising phantoms flitting by the door."

Nan led the way, and the two pyramids revolved before him with the rapidity of lay-figures, much to the good man's edification: for with his fatherly pleasure there was mingled much mild wonderment at the amplitude of array.

"Yes, I see my geese are really swans, though there is such a cloud between us that I feel a long way off, and hardly know them. But this little daughter is always available, always my 'cricket on the hearth.'"

As he spoke, her father drew Nan closer, kissed her tranquil face, and smiled content.

"Well, if ever I see picters, I see 'em now, and I declare to goodness it's as interestin' as playactin', every bit. Miss Di with all them boughs in her head, looks like the Queen of Sheby, when she went a-visitin' What's-his-name; and if Miss Laura ain't as sweet as a lally-barster figger, I should like to know what is."

In her enthusiasm, Sally gambolled about the girls, flourishing her

23

milk-pan like a modern Miriam about to sound her timbrel for excess of joy.

Laughing merrily, the two Mont Blancs bestowed themselves in the family ark, Nan hopped up beside Patrick, and Solon, roused from his lawful slumbers, morosely trundled them away. But, looking backward with a last "Good-night!" Nan saw her father still standing at the door with smiling countenance, and the moonlight falling like a benediction on his silver hair.

"Betsey shall go up the hill with you, my dear, and here's a basket of eggs for your father. Give him my love, and be sure you let me know the next time he is poorly," Mrs. Lord said, when her guest rose to depart, after an hour of pleasant chat.

But Nan never got the gift; for, to her great dismay, her hostess dropped the basket with a crash, and flew across the room to meet a tall shape pausing in the shadow of the door. There was no need to ask who the new-comer was; for, even in his mother's arms, John looked over her shoulder with an eager nod to Nan, who stood among the ruins with never a sign of weariness in her face, nor the memory of a care at her heart.—for they all went out when John came in.

"Now tell us how and why and when you came. Take off your coat, my dear! And here are the old slippers. Why didn't you let us know you were coming so soon? How have you been? and what makes you so late to-night? Betsey, you needn't put on your bonnet. And—oh, my dear boy, have you been to supper yet?"

Mrs. Lord was a quiet soul, and her flood of questions was purred softly in her son's ear; for, being a woman, she must talk, and, being a mother, must pet the one delight of her life, and make a little festival when the lord of the manor came home. A whole drove of fatted calves were metaphorically killed, and a banquet appeared with speed.

John was not one of those romantic heroes who can go through three volumes of hair-breadth escapes without the faintest hint of that blessed institution, dinner; therefore, like "Lady Letherbridge," he partook, copiously of everything, while the two women beamed over each mouthful with an interest that enhanced its flavor, and urged upon him cold meat and cheese, pickles and pie, as if dyspepsia and nightmare were among the lost arts.

Then he opened his budget of news and fed them.

"I was coming next month, according to custom; but Philip fell upon and so tempted me, that I was driven to sacrifice myself to the cause of friendship, and up we came to-night. He would not let me come here till we had seen your father, Nan; for the poor lad was pining for Laura, and hoped his good behavior for the past year would satisfy his judge and secure his recall. We had a fine talk with your father; and, upon my life, Philip seemed to have received the gift of tongues, for he made a most eloquent plea, which I've stored away for future use, I assure you. The dear old gentleman was very kind, told Phil he was satisfied with the success of his probation, that he should see Laura when he liked, and, if all went well, should receive his reward in the spring. It must be a delightful sensation to know you have made a fellow-creature as happy as those words made Phil to-night."

John paused, and looked musingly at the matronly tea-pot, as if he saw a wondrous future in its shine.

Nan twinkled off the drops that rose at the thought of Laura's joy, and said, with grateful warmth, —

25

"You say nothing of your own share in the making of that happiness, John; but we know it, for Philip has told Laura in his letters all that you have been to him, and I am sure there was other eloquence beside his own before father granted all you say he has. Oh, John, I thank you very much for this!"

Mrs. Lord beamed a whole midsummer of delight upon her son, as she saw the pleasure these words gave him, though he answered simply,—

"I only tried to be a brother to him, Nan; for he has been most kind to me. Yes, I said my little say to-night, and gave my testimony in behalf of the prisoner at the bar; a most merciful judge pronounced his sentence, and he rushed straight to Mrs. Leigh's to tell Laura the blissful news. Just imagine the scene when he appears, and how Di will open her wicked eyes and enjoy the spectacle of the dishevelled lover, the bride-elect's tears, the stir, and the romance of the thing. She'll cry over it to-night, and caricature it to-morrow."

And John led the laugh at the picture he had conjured up, to turn the thoughts of Di's dangerous sister from himself.

At ten Nan retired into the depths of her old bonnet with a far different face from the one she brought out of it, and John, resuming his hat, mounted guard.

"Don't stay late, remember, John!" And in Mrs. Lord's voice there was a warning tone that her son interpreted aright.

"I'll not forget, mother."

And he kept his word; for though Philip's happiness floated temptingly before him, and the little figure at his side had never seemed so dear, he ignored the bland winds, the tender night, and set a seal upon his lips, thinking manfully within himself. "I see many signs of promise in her happy face; but I will wait and hope a little longer for her sake."

"Where is father, Sally?" asked Nan, as that functionary appeared, blinking owlishly, but utterly repudiating the idea of sleep.

"He went down the garding, miss, when the gentlemen cleared, bein' a little flustered by the goin's on. Shall I fetch him in?" asked Sally, as irreverently as if her master were a bag of meal.

"No, we will go ourselves." And slowly the two paced down the leaf-strewn walk.

Fields of yellow grain were waving on the hill-side, and sere corn blades rustled in the wind, from the orchard came the scent of ripening fruit, and all the garden-plots lay ready to yield up their humble offerings to their master's hand. But in the silence of the night a greater Reaper had passed by, gathering in the harvest of a righteous life, and leaving only tender memories for the gleaners who had come so late.

The old man sat in the shadow of the tree his own hands planted; its fruit boughs shone ruddily, and its leaves still whispered the low lullaby that hushed him to his rest.

"How fast he sleeps! Poor father! I should have come before and made it pleasant for him."

As she spoke, Nan lifted up the head bent down upon his breast, and kissed his pallid cheek.

"Oh, John, this is not sleep."

"Yes, dear, the happiest he will ever know."

For a moment the shadows flickered over three white faces and the silence deepened solemnly. Then John reverently bore the pale shape in, and Nan dropped down beside it, saying, with a rain of grateful tears,—

"He kissed me when I went, and said a last good-night!'"

For an hour steps went to and fro about her, many voices whispered near her, and skilful hands touched the beloved clay she held so fast; but one by one the busy feet passed out, one by one the voices died away, and human skill proved vain.

Then Mrs. Lord drew the orphan to the shelter of her arms, soothing her with the mute solace of that motherly embrace.

"Nan, Nan! here's Philip! come and see!" The happy call re-echoed through the house, and Nan sprang up as if her time for grief were past.

"I must tell them. Oh, my poor girls, how will they bear it?—they have known so little sorrow!"

But there was no need for her to speak; other lips had spared her the hard task. For, as she stirred to meet them, a sharp cry rent the air, steps rang upon the stairs, and two wild-eyed creatures came into the hush of that familiar room, for the first time meeting with no welcome from their father's voice.

With one impulse, Di and Laura fled to Nan, and the sisters clung together in a silent embrace, more eloquent than words. John took his mother by the hand, and led her from the room, closing the door upon the sacredness of grief.

"Yes, we are poorer than we thought; but when everything is

settled, we shall get on very well. We can let a part of this great house, and live quietly together until spring; then Laura will be married, and Di can go on their travels with them, as Philip wishes her to do. We shall be cared for; so never fear for us, John."

Nan said this, as her friend parted from her a week later, after the saddest holiday he had ever known.

"And what becomes of you, Nan?" he asked, watching the patient eyes that smiled when others would have wept.

"I shall stay in the dear old house; for no other place would seem like home to me. I shall find some little child to love and care for, and be quite happy till the girls come back and want me."

John nodded wisely, as he listened, and went away prophesying within himself,—

"She shall find something more than a child to love; and, God willing, shall be very happy till the girls come home and—cannot have her."

Nan's plan was carried into effect. Slowly the divided waters closed again, and the three fell back into their old life. But the touch of sorrow drew them closer; and, though invisible, a beloved presence still moved among them, a familiar voice still spoke to them in the silence of their softened hearts. Thus the soil was made ready, and in the depth of winter the good seed was sown, was watered with many tears, and soon sprang up green with a promise of a harvest for their after years.

Di and Laura consoled themselves with their favorite employments, unconscious that Nan was growing paler, thinner, and more silent, as the weeks went by, till one day she dropped quietly before them, and it suddenly became manifest that she was utterly worn out with many cares and the secret suffering of a tender heart bereft of the paternal love which had been its strength and stay.

"I'm only tired, dear girls. Don't be troubled, for I shall be up to-morrow," she said cheerily, as she looked into the anxious faces bending over her.

But the weariness was of many months' growth, and it was weeks before that "to-morrow" came.

Laura installed herself as nurse, and her devotion was repaid four-fold; for, sitting at her sister's bedside, she learned a finer art than that she had left. Her eye grew clear to see the beauty of a self-denying life, and in the depths of Nan's meek nature she found the strong, sweet virtues that made her what she was.

Then remembering that these womanly attributes were a bride's best dowry, Laura gave herself to their attainment, that she might become to another household the blessing Nan had been to her own; and turning from the worship of the goddess Beauty, she gave her hand to that humbler and more human teacher, Duty,— learning her lessons with a willing heart, for Philip's sake.

Di corked her inkstand, locked her bookcase, and went at housework as if it were a five-barred gate; of course she missed the leap, but scrambled bravely through, and appeared much sobered by the exercise. Sally had departed to sit under a vine and fig-tree of her own, so Di had undisputed sway; but if dish-pans and dusters had tongues, direful would have been the history of that crusade against frost and fire, indolence and inexperience. But they were dumb, and Di scorned to complain, though her struggles were pathetic to behold, and her sisters went through a series of messes

30

equal to a course of "Prince Benreddin's" peppery tarts. Reality turned Romance out of doors; for, unlike her favorite heroines in satin and tears, or helmet and shield, Di met her fate in a big checked apron and dust-cap, wonderful to see; yet she wielded her broom as stoutly as "Moll Pitcher" shouldered her gun, and marched to her daily martyrdom in the kitchen with as heroic a heart as the "Maid of Orleans" took to her stake.

Mind won the victory over matter in the end, and Di was better all her days for the tribulations and the triumphs of that time; for she drowned her idle fancies in her wash-tub, made burnt-offerings of selfishness and pride, and learned the worth of self-denial, as she sang with happy voice among the pots and kettles of her conquered realm.

Nan thought of John, and in the stillness of her sleepless nights prayed Heaven to keep him safe, and make her worthy to receive and strong enough to bear the blessedness or pain of love.

Snow fell without, and keen winds howled among the leafless elms, but "herbs of grace" were blooming beautifully in the sunshine of sincere endeavor, and this dreariest season proved the most fruitful of the year; for love taught Laura, labor chastened Di, and patience fitted Nan for the blessing of her life.

Nature, that stillest, yet most diligent of housewives, began at last that "spring cleaning" which she makes so pleasant that none find the heart to grumble as they do when other matrons set their premises a-dust. Her hand-maids, wind and rain and sun, swept, washed, and garnished busily, green carpets were unrolled, apple-boughs were hung with draperies of bloom, and dandelions, pet nurslings of the year, came out to play upon the sward.

From the South returned that opera troupe whose manager is never in despair, whose tenor never sulks, whose prima donna never fails, and in the orchard bona fide matinees were held, to which buttercups and clovers crowded in their prettiest spring hats, and verdant young blades twinkled their dewy lorgnettes, as they bowed and made way for the floral belles.

May was bidding June good-morrow, and the roses were just dreaming that it was almost time to wake, when John came again into the quiet room which now seemed the Eden that contained his Eve. Of course there was a jubilee; but something seemed to have befallen the whole group, for never had they appeared in such odd frames of mind. John was restless, and wore an excited look, most unlike his usual serenity of aspect.

Nan the cheerful had fallen into a well of silence and was not to be extracted by any Hydraulic power, though she smiled like the June sky over her head. Di's peculiarities were out in full force, and she looked as if she would go off like a torpedo at a touch; but through all her moods there was a half-triumphant, half-remorseful expression in the glance she fixed on John. And Laura, once so silent, now sang like a blackbird, as she flitted to and fro; but her fitful song was always, "Philip, my king."

John felt that there had come a change upon the three, and silently divined whose unconscious influence had wrought the miracle. The embargo was off his tongue, and he was in a fever to ask that question which brings a flutter to the stoutest heart; but though the "man" had come, the "hour" had not. So, by way of steadying his nerves, he paced the room, pausing often to take notes of his companions, and each pause seemed to increase his wonder and content.

He looked at Nan. She was in her usual place, the rigid little chair she loved, because it once was large enough to hold a curly-headed playmate and herself. The old work-basket was at her side, and the battered thimble busily at work; but her lips wore a smile they had never worn before, the color of the unblown roses touched her cheek, and her downcast eyes were full of light.

He looked at Di. The inevitable book was on her knee, but its leaves were uncut; the strong-minded knob of hair still asserted its supremacy aloft upon her head, and the triangular jacket still adorned her shoulders in defiance of all fashions, past, present, or to come; but the expression of her brown countenance had grown softer, her tongue had found a curb, and in her hand lay a card with "Potts, Kettel & Co." inscribed thereon, which she regarded with never a scornful word for the "Co."

He looked at Laura. She was before her easel as of old; but the pale nun had given place to a blooming girl, who sang at her work, which was no prim Pallas, but a Clytie turning her human face to meet the sun.

"John, what are you thinking of?"

He stirred as if Di's voice had disturbed his fancy at some pleasant pastime, but answered with his usual sincerity, —

"I was thinking of a certain dear old fairy tale called 'Cinderella.'"

"Oh!" said Di; and her "Oh" was a most impressive monosyllable. "I see the meaning of your smile now; and though the application of the story is not very complimentary to all parties concerned, it is very just and very true."

She paused a moment, then went on with softened voice and earnest mien: —

"You think I am a blind and selfish creature. So I am, but not so blind and selfish as I have been; for many tears have cleared my eyes, and much sincere regret has made me humbler than I was. I have found a better book than any father's library can give me, and I have read it with a love and admiration that grew stronger as I turned the leaves. Henceforth I take it for my guide and gospel, and, looking back upon the selfish and neglectful past, can only say, Heaven bless your dear heart, Nan!"

Laura echoed Di's last words; for, with eyes as full of tenderness, she looked down upon the sister she had lately learned to know, saying, warmly,—

"Yes, 'Heaven bless your dear heart, Nan!' I never can forget all you have been to me; and when I am far away with Philip, there will always be one countenance more beautiful to me than any pictured face I may discover, there will be one place more dear to me than Rome. The face will be yours, Nan, always so patient, always so serene; and the dearer place will be this home of ours, which you have made so pleasant to me all these years by kindnesses as numberless and noiseless as the drops of dew."

"Dear girls, what have I ever done, that you should love me so?" cried Nan, with happy wonderment, as the tall heads, black and golden, bent to meet the lowly brown one, and her sisters' mute lips answered her.

Then Laura looked up, saying, playfully,—

"Here are the good and wicked sisters;-where shall we find the Prince?"

"There!" cried Di, pointing to John; and then her secret went off like a rocket; for, with her old impetuosity, she said,—

34

"I have found you out, John, and am ashamed to look you in the face, remembering the past. Girls, you know when father died, John sent us money, which he said Mr. Owen had long owed us and had paid at last? It was a kind lie, John, and a generous thing to do; for we needed it, but never would have taken it as a gift. I know you meant that we should never find this out; but yesterday I met Mr. Owen returning from the West, and when I thanked him for a piece of justice we had not expected of him, he gruffly told me he had never paid the debt, never meant to pay it, for it was outlawed, and we could not claim a farthing. John, I have laughed at you, thought you stupid, treated you unkindly; but I know you now, and never shall forget the lesson you have taught me. I am proud as Lucifer, but I ask you to forgive me, and I seal my real repentance so—and so."

With tragic countenance, Di rushed across the room, threw both arms about the astonished young man's neck and dropped an energetic kiss upon his cheek. There was a momentary silence; for Di finally illustrated her strong-minded theories by crying like the weakest of her sex. Laura, with "the ruling passion strong in death," still tried to draw, but broke her pet crayon, and endowed her Clytie with a supplementary orb, owing to the dimness of her own. And Nan sat with drooping eyes, that shone upon her work, thinking with tender pride,—"They know him now, and love him for his generous heart."

Di spoke first, rallying to her colors, though a little daunted by her loss of self-control.

"Don't laugh, John,—I couldn't help it; and don't think I'm not sincere, for I am,—I am; and I will prove it by growing good enough to be your friend. That debt must all be paid, and I shall do it; for I'll turn my books and pen to some account, and write stories full of clear old souls like you and Nan; and some one, I know, will like and buy them, though they are not 'works of Shakespeare.' I've thought of this before, have felt I had the power in me; now I have the motive, and now I'll do it."

If Di had Proposed to translate the Koran, or build a new Saint Paul's, there would have been many chances of success; for, once moved, her will, like a battering-ram, would knock down the obstacles her wits could not surmount. John believed in her most heartily, and showed it, as he answered, looking into her resolute face, —

"I know you will, and yet make us very proud of our 'Chaos,' Di. Let the money lie, and when you have a fortune, I'll claim it with enormous interest; but, believe me, I feel already doubly repaid by the esteem so generously confessed, so cordially bestowed, and can only say, as we used to years ago, — 'Now let's forgive and so forget."

But proud Di would not let him add to her obligation, even by returning her impetuous salute; she slipped away, and, shaking off the last drops, answered with a curious mixture of old freedom and new respect, —

"No more sentiment, please, John. We know each other now; and when I find a friend, I never let him go. We have smoked the pipe of peace; so let us go back to our wigwams and bury the feud. Where were we when I lost my head? and what were we talking about?"

"Cinderella and the Prince."

As she spoke, John's eye kindled, and, turning, he looked down at

36

Nan, who sat diligently ornamenting with microscopic stitches a great patch going on, the wrong side out.

"Yes,—so we were; and now taking pussy for the godmother, the characters of the story are well personated,—all but the slipper," said Di, laughing, as she thought of the many times they had played it together years ago.

A sudden movement stirred John's frame, a sudden purpose shone in his countenance, and a sudden change befell his voice, as he said, producing from some hiding-place a little wornout shoe,—

"I can supply the slipper;—who will try it first?"

Di's black eyes opened wide, as they fell on the familiar object; then her romance-loving nature saw the whole plot of that drama which needs but two to act it. A great delight flushed up into her face, as she promptly took her cue, saying—

"No need for us to try it, Laura; for it wouldn't fit us, if our feet were as small as Chinese dolls; our parts are played out; therefore 'Exeunt wicked sisters to the music of the wedding-bells.'"

And pouncing upon the dismayed artist, she swept her out and closed the door with a triumphant bang.

John went to Nan, and, dropping on his knee as reverently as the herald of the fairy tale, he asked, still smiling, but with lips grown tremulous,—

"Will Cinderella try the little shoe, and—if it fits—go with the Prince?"

But Nan only covered up her face, weeping happy tears, while all the weary work strayed down upon the floor, as if it knew her holiday had come.

John drew the hidden face still closer, and while she listened to his eager words, Nan heard the beating of the strong man's heart, and knew it spoke the truth.

"Nan, I promised mother to be silent till I was sure I loved you wholly,—sure that the knowledge would give no pain when I should tell it, as I am trying to tell it now. This little shoe has been my comforter through this long year, and I have kept it as other lovers keep their fairer favors. It has been a talisman more eloquent to me than flower or ring; for, when I saw how worn it was, I always thought of the willing feet that came and went for others' comfort all day long; when I saw the little bow you tied, I always thought of the hands so diligent in serving any one who knew a want or felt a pain; and when I recalled the gentle creature who had worn it last, I always saw her patient, tender, and devout,—and tried to grow more worthy of her, that I might one day dare to ask if she would walk beside me all my life and be my 'angel in the house.' Will you, dear? Believe me, you shall never know a weariness or grief I have the power to shield you from."

Then Nan, as simple in her love as in her life, laid her arms about his neck, her happy face against his own, and answered softly,—

"Oh, John, I never can be sad or tired any more!"

DEBBY'S DEBUT

On a cheery June day Mrs. Penelope Carroll and her niece Debby Wilder, were whizzing along on their way to a certain gay watering-place, both in the best of humors with each other and all the world beside. Aunt Pen was concocting sundry mild romances, and laying harmless plots for the pursuance of her favorite pastime, match-making; for she had invited her pretty relative to join her summer jaunt, ostensibly that the girl might see a little of fashionable life, but the good lady secretly proposed to herself to take her to the beach and get her a rich husband, very much as she would have proposed to take her to Broadway and get her a new bonnet: for both articles she considered necessary, but somewhat difficult for a poor girl to obtain.

Debby was slowly getting her poise, after the excitement of a first visit to New York; for ten days of bustle had introduced the young philosopher to a new existence, and the working-day world seemed to have vanished when she made her last pat of butter in the dairy at home. For an hour she sat thinking over the good-fortune which had befallen her, and the comforts of this life which she had suddenly acquired. Debby was a true girl, with all a girl's love of ease and pleasure; it must not be set down against her that she surveyed her pretty travelling-suit with much complacency, rejoicing inwardly that she could use her hands without exposing fractured gloves, that her bonnet was of the newest mode, needing no veil to hide a faded ribbon or a last year's shape, that her dress swept the ground with fashionable untidiness, and her boots were guiltless of a patch,—that she was the possessor of a mine of wealth in two of the eight trunks belonging to her aunt, that she was travelling like any lady of the land with man- and maid-servant at her command, and that she was leaving work and care behind her for a month or two of novelty and rest.

When these agreeable facts were fully realized, and Aunt Pen had fallen asleep behind her veil, Debby took out a book, and indulged in her favorite luxury, soon forgetting past, present, and future in the inimitable history of Martin Chuzzlewit. The sun blazed, the cars rattled, children cried, ladies nodded, gentlemen longed for the solace of prohibited cigars, and newspapers were converted into sun-shades, nightcaps, and fans; but Debby read on, unconscious of all about her, even of the pair of eves that watched her from the Opposite corner of the car. A Gentleman with a frank, strong-featured face sat therein, and amused himself by scanning with thoughtful gaze the countenances of his fellow-travellers. Stout Aunt Pen, dignified even in her sleep, was a "model of deportment" to the rising generation; but the student of human nature found a more attractive subject in her companion, the girl with an apple-blossom face and merry brown eyes, who sat smiling into her book, never heeding that her bonnet was awry, and the wind taking unwarrantable liberties with her ribbons and her hair.

Innocent Debby turned her pages, unaware that her fate sat opposite in the likeness of a serious, black-bearded gentleman, who watched the smiles rippling from her lips to her eyes with an interest that deepened as the minutes passed. If his paper had been full of anything but "Bronchial Troches" and "Spalding's Prepared Glue," he would have found more profitable employment; but it wasn't, and with the usual readiness of idle souls he fell into evil ways, and permitted curiosity, that feminine sin, to enter in and take possession of his manly mind. A great desire seized him to

40

discover what book his pretty neighbor; but a cover hid the name, and he was too distant to catch it on the fluttering leaves. Presently a stout Emerald-Islander, with her wardrobe oozing out of sundry paper parcels, vacated the seat behind the two ladies; and it was soon quietly occupied by the individual for whom Satan was finding such indecorous employment. Peeping round the little gray bonnet, past a brown braid and a fresh cheek, the young man's eye fell upon the words the girl was reading, and forgot to look away again. Books were the desire of his life; but an honorable purpose and an indomitable will kept him steady at his ledgers till he could feel that he had earned the right to read. Like wine to many another was an open page to his; he read a line, and, longing for more, took a hasty sip from his neighbor's cup, forgetting that it was a stranger's also.

Down the page went the two pairs of eyes, and the merriment from Debby's seemed to light up the sombre ones behind her with a sudden shine that softened the whole face and made it very winning. No wonder they twinkled, for Elijah Pogram spoke, and "Mrs. Hominy, the mother of the modern Gracchi, in the classical blue cap and the red cotton pocket-handkerchief, came down the room in a procession of one." A low laugh startled Debby, though it was smothered like the babes in the Tower; and, turning, she beheld the trespasser scarlet with confusion, and sobered with a tardy sense of his transgression. Debby was not a starched young lady of the "prune and prism" school, but a frank, free-hearted little body, quick to read the sincerity of others, and to take looks and words at their real value. Dickens was her idol; and for his sake she could have forgiven a greater offence than this.

The stranger's contrite countenance and respectful apology won her good-will at once; and with a finer courtesy than any Aunt Pen would have taught, she smilingly bowed her pardon, and, taking another book from her basket, opened it, saying, pleasantly, —

"Here is the first volume if you like it, Sir. I can recommend it as an invaluable consolation for the discomforts of a summer day's journey, and it is heartily at your service."

As much surprised as gratified, the gentleman accepted the book, and retired behind it with the sudden discovery that wrongdoing has its compensation in the pleasurable sensation of being forgiven. Stolen delights are well known to be specially saccharine: and much as this pardoned sinner loved books, it seemed to him that the interest of the story flagged, and that the enjoyment of reading was much enhanced by the proximity of a gray bonnet and a girlish profile. But Dickens soon proved more powerful than Debby, and she was forgotten, till, pausing to turn a leaf, the young man met her shy glance, as she asked, with the pleased expression of a child who has shared an apple with a playmate, —

"Is it good?"

"Oh, very!"—and the man looked as honestly grateful for the book as the boy would have done for the apple.

Only five words in the conversation, but Aunt Pen woke, as if the watchful spirit of propriety had roused her to pluck her charge from the precipice on which she stood.

"Dora, I'm astonished at you! Speaking to strangers in that free manner is a most unladylike thing. How came you to forget what I have told you over and over again about a proper reserve?" The energetic whisper reached the gentleman's ear, and he expected to be annihilated with a look when his offence was revealed; but he was spared that ordeal, for the young voice answered, softly, —

"Don't faint, Aunt Pen: I only did as I'd be done by; for I had two books, and the poor man looked so hungry for something to read that I couldn't resist sharing my 'goodies.' He will see that I'm a countrified little thing in spite of my fine feathers, and won't be shocked at my want of rigidity and frigidity; so don't look dismal, and I'll be prim and proper all the rest of the way,—if I don't forget it."

"I wonder who he is; may belong to some of our first families, and in that case it might be worth while to exert ourselves, you know. Did you learn his name, Dora?" whispered the elder lady.

Debby shook her head, and murmured, "Hush!"—but Aunt Pen had heard of matches being made in cars as well as in heaven; and as an experienced general, it became her to reconnoitre, when one of the enemy approached her camp. Slightly altering her position, she darted an all-comprehensive glance at the invader, who seemed entirely absorbed, for not an eyelash stirred during the scrutiny. It lasted but an instant, yet in that instant he was weighed and found wanting; for that experienced eye detected that his cravat was two inches wider than fashion ordained, that his coat was not of the latest style, that his gloves were mended, and his handkerchief neither cambric nor silk. That was enough, and sentence was passed forthwith,—"Some respectable clerk, good-looking, but poor, and not at all the thing for Dora"; and Aunt Pen turned to adjust a voluminous green veil over her niece's bonnet, "To shield it from the dust, dear," which process also shielded the face within from the eye of man.

A curious smile, half mirthful, half melancholy, passed over their neighbor's lips; but his peace of mind seemed undisturbed, and he remained buried in his book Till they reached — —, at dusk. As he returned it, he offered his services in procuring a carriage or attending to luggage; but Mrs. Carroll, with much dignity of aspect, informed him that her servants would attend to those matters, and, bowing gravely, he vanished into the night.

As they rolled away to the hotel, Debby was wild to run down to the beach whence came the solemn music of the sea, making the twilight beautiful. But Aunt Pen was too tired to do anything but sup in her own apartment and go early to bed; and Debby might as soon have proposed to walk up the great Pyramid as to make her first appearance without that sage matron to mount guard over her; so she resigned herself to pie and patience, and fell asleep, wishing it were to-morrow.

At five, a. m., a nightcapped head appeared at one of the myriad windows of the — — Hotel, and remained there as if fascinated by the miracle of sunrise over the sea. Under her simplicity of character and girlish merriment Debby possessed a devout spirit and a nature full of the real poetry of life, two gifts that gave her dawning womanhood its sweetest charm, and made her what she was. As she looked out that summer dawn upon the royal marriage of the ocean and the sun, all petty hopes and longings faded out of sight, and her young face grew luminous with thoughts too deep for words. Her day was happier for that silent hour, her life richer for the aspirations that uplifted her like beautiful strong angels, and left a blessing when they went. The smile of the June sky touched her lips, the morning red seemed to linger on her cheek, and in her eye arose a light kindled by the shimmer of that broad sea of gold; for Nature rewarded her young votary well, and gave her beauty, when she offered love. How long she leaned there Debby did not know; steps from below roused her from her reverie, and led her back into the world again. Smiling at herself, She stole to bed, and lay wrapped in waking dreams as changeful as the shadows, dancing on her chamber-wall.

The advent of her aunt's maid, Victorine, some two hours later, was the signal to be "up and doing"; and she meekly resigned herself into the hands of that functionary, who appeared to regard her in the light of an animated pin-cushion, as she performed the toilet-ceremonies with an absorbed aspect, which impressed her subject with a sense of the solemnity of the occasion.

"Now, Mademoiselle, regard yourself, and pronounce that you are ravishing," Victorine said at length, folding her hands with a sigh of satisfaction, as she fell back in an attitude of serene triumph.

Debby obeyed, and inspected herself with great interest and some astonishment; for there was a sweeping amplitude of array about the young lady whom she beheld in the much-befrilled gown and embroidered skirts, which somewhat alarmed her as to the navigation of a vessel "with such a spread of sail," while a curious sensation of being somebody else pervaded her from the crown of her head, with its shining coils of hair, to the soles of the French slippers, whose energies seemed to have been devoted to the production of marvellous rosettes.

"Yes, I look very nice, thank you; and yet I feel like a doll, helpless and fine, and fancy I was more of a woman in my fresh gingham, with a knot of clovers in my hair, than I am now. Aunt Pen was very kind to get me all these pretty things; but I'm afraid my mother would look horrified to see me in such a high state of flounce externally and so little room to breath internally."

"Your mamma would not flatter me, Mademoiselle; but come now to Madame; she is waiting to behold you, and I have yet her toilet to make "; and, with a pitying shrug, Victorine followed Debby to her aunt's room.

45

"Charming! really elegant!" cried that lady, emerging from her towel with a rubicund visage.

"Drop that braid half an inch lower, and pull the worked end of her handkerchief out of the right-hand pocket, Vic. There! Now, Dora, don't run about and get rumpled, but sit quietly down and practice repose till I am ready."

Debby obeyed, and sat mute, with the air of a child in its Sunday-best on a week-day, pleased with the novelty, but somewhat oppressed with the responsibility of such unaccustomed splendor, and utterly unable to connect any ideas of repose with tight shoes and skirts in a rampant state of starch.

"Well, you see, I bet on Lady Gay against Cockadoodle, and if you'll believe me—Hullo! there's Mrs. Carroll, and deuse take me if she hasn't got a girl with her! Look, Seguin!"—and Joe Leavenworth, a "man of the world," aged twenty, paused in his account of an exciting race to make the announcement.

Mr. Seguin, his friend and Mentor, as much his, senior in worldly wickedness as in years, tore himself from his breakfast long enough to survey the new-comers, and then returned to it, saying, briefly,—

"The old lady is worth cultivating,—gives good suppers, and thanks you for eating them. The girl is well got up, but has no style, and blushes like a milkmaid. Better fight shy of her, Joe."

"Do you think so? Well, now I rather fancy that kind of thing. She's new, you see, and I get on with that sort of girl the best, for the old ones are so deused knowing that a fellow has no chance of a—By the Lord Harry, she's eating bread and milk!"

Young Leavenworth whisked his glass into his eye, and Mr. Seguin

46

put down his roll to behold the phenomenon. Poor Debby! her first step had been a wrong one.

All great minds have their weak points. Aunt Pen's was her breakfast, and the peace of her entire day depended upon the success of that meal. Therefore, being down rather late, the worthy lady concentrated her energies upon the achievement of a copious repast, and, trusting to former lessons, left Debby to her own resources for a few fatal moments. After the flutter occasioned by being scooped into her seat by a severe-nosed waiter, Debby had only courage enough left to refuse tea and coffee and accept milk. That being done, she took the first familiar viand that appeared, and congratulated herself upon being able to get her usual breakfast. With returning composure, she looked about her and began to enjoy the buzz of voices, the clatter of knives and forks, and the long lines of faces all intent upon the business of the hour; but her peace was of short duration. Pausing for a fresh relay of toast, Aunt Pen glanced toward her niece with the comfortable conviction that her appearance was highly creditable; and her dismay can be imagined, when she beheld that young lady placidly devouring a great cup of brown-bread and milk before the eyes of the assembled multitude. The poor lady choked in her coffee, and between her gasps whispered irefully behind her napkin,—

"For Heaven's sake, Dora, put away that mess! The Ellenboroughs are directly opposite, watching everything you do. Eat that omelet, or anything respectable, unless you want me to die of mortification."

Debby dropped her spoon, and, hastily helping herself from the dish her aunt pushed toward her, consumed the leathery compound with as much grace as she could assume, though unable to repress a laugh at Aunt Pen's disturbed countenance. There was a slight lull in the clatter, and the blithe sound caused several heads to turn toward the quarter whence it came, for it was as unexpected and pleasant a sound as a bobolink's song in a cage of shrill-voiced canaries.

"She's a jolly little thing and powerful pretty, so deuse take me if I don't make up to the old lady and find out who the girl is. I've been introduced to Mrs. Carroll at our house: but I suppose she won't remember me till I remind her."

The "deuse" declining to accept of his repeated offers (probably because there was still too much honor and honesty in the boy,) young Leavenworth sought out Mrs. Carroll on the Piazza, as she and Debby were strolling there an hour later.

"Joe Leavenworth, my dear, from one of our first families,—very wealthy,—fine match,—pray, be civil,—smooth your hair, hold back your shoulders, and put down your parasol," murmured Aunt Pen, as the gentleman approached with as much pleasure in his countenance as it was consistent with manly dignity to express upon meeting two of the inferior race.

"My niece, Miss Dora Wilder. This is her first season at the beach, and we must endeavor to make it pleasant for her, or she will be getting homesick and running away to mamma," said Aunt Pen, in her society-tone, after she had returned his greeting, and perpetrated a polite fiction, by declaring that she remembered him perfectly, for he was the image of his father.

Mr. Leavenworth brought the heels of his varnished boots together with a click, and executed the latest bow imported, then stuck his glass in his eye and stared till it fell out, (the glass, not the eye,) upon which he fell into step with them, remarking,—

"I shall be most happy to show the lions: they are deused tame ones, so you needn't be alarmed. Miss Wilder."

Debby was good-natured enough to laugh; and, elated with that success, he proceeded to pour forth his stores of wit and learning in true collegian style, quite unconscious that the "jolly little thing" was looking him through and through with the smiling eyes that were producing such pleasurable sensations under the mosaic studs. They strolled toward the beach, and, meeting an old acquaintance, Aunt Pen fell behind, and beamed upon the young pair as if her prophetic eye even at this early stage beheld them walking altarward in a proper state of blond white vest and bridal awkwardness.

"Can you skip a stone, Mr. Leavenworth? asked Debby, possessed with a mischievous desire to shock the piece of elegance at her side.

"Eh? what's that?" he inquired, with his head on one side, like an inquisitive robin.

Debby repeated her question, and illustrated it by sending a stone skimming over the water in the most scientific manner. Mr. Joe was painfully aware that this was not at all "the thing," that his sisters never did so, and that Seguin would laugh confoundedly, if he caught him at it; but Debby looked so irresistibly fresh and pretty under her rose-lined parasol that he was moved to confess that he had done such a thing, and to sacrifice his gloves by poking in the sand, that he might indulge in a like unfashionable pastime.

"You'll be at the hop to-night, I hope, Miss Wilder," he observed, introducing a topic suited to a young lady's mental capacity.

"Yes, indeed; for dancing is one of the joys of my life, next to husking and making hay"; and Debby polked a few steps along the beach, much to the edification of a pair of old gentlemen, serenely taking their first constitutional.

"Making what?" cried Mr. Joe, poking after her.

"Hay; ah, that is the pleasantest fun in the world,—and better exercise, my mother says, for soul and body, than dancing till dawn in crowded rooms, with everything in a state of unnatural excitement. If one wants real merriment, let him go into a new-mown field, where all the air is full of summer odors, where wild-flowers nod along the walls, where blackbirds make finer music than any band, and sun and wind and cheery voices do their part, while windrows rise, and great loads go rumbling through the lanes with merry brown faces atop. Yes, much as I like dancing, it is not to be compared with that; for in the one case we shut out the lovely world, and in the other we become a part of it, till by its magic labor turns to poetry, and we harvest something better than dried buttercups and grass."

As she spoke, Debby looked up, expecting to meet a glance of disapproval; but something in the simple earnestness of her manner had recalled certain boyish pleasures as innocent as they were hearty, which now contrasted very favorably with the later pastimes in which fast horses, and that lower class of animals, fast men, bore so large a part. Mr. Joe thoughtfully punched five holes in the sand, and for a moment Debby liked the expression of his face; then the old listlessness returned, and, looking up, he said, with an air of ennui that was half sad, half ludicrous, in one so young and so generously endowed with youth, health, and the good gifts of this life,—

"I used to fancy that sort of thing years ago, but I'm afraid I should find it a little slow now, though you describe it in such an inviting manner that I would be tempted to try it, if a hay-cock came in my way; for, upon my life, it's deused heavy work loafing about at these watering-places all summer. Between ourselves, there's a deal of humbug about this kind of life, as you will find, when you've tried it as long as I have."

"Yes, I begin to think so already; but perhaps you can give me a few friendly words of warning from the stones of your experience, that I may be spared the pain of saying what so many look, — 'Grandma, the world is hollow; my doll is stuffed with sawdust; and I should 'like to go into a convent, if you please.'"

Debby's eyes were dancing with merriment; but they were demurely down-cast, and her voice was perfectly serious.

The milk of human kindness had been slightly curdled for Mr. Joe by sundry college-tribulations; and having been "suspended," he very naturally vibrated between the inborn jollity of his temperament and the bitterness occasioned by his wrongs.

He had lost at billiards the night before, had been hurried at breakfast, had mislaid his cigar-case, and splashed his boots; consequently the darker mood prevailed that morning, and when his counsel was asked, he gave it like one who bad known the heaviest trials of this "Piljin Projiss of a wale."

"There's no justice in the world, no chance for us young people to enjoy ourselves, without some penalty to pay, some drawback to worry us like these confounded 'all-rounders.' Even here, where all seems free and easy, there's no end of gossips and spies who tattle and watch till you feel as if you lived in a lantern. 'Every one for himself, and the Devil take the hindmost'; that's the principle they go on, and you have to keep your wits about you in the most

51

exhausting manner, or you are done for before you know it. I've seen a good deal of this sort of thing, and hope you'll get on better than some do, when it's known that you are the rich Mrs. Carroll's niece; though you don't need that fact to enhance your charms,— upon my life, you don't."

Debby laughed behind her parasol at this burst of candor; but her independent nature prompted her to make a fair beginning, in spite of Aunt Pen's polite fictions and well-meant plans.

"Thank you for your warning, but I don't apprehend much annoyance of that kind," she said, demurely. "Do you know, I think, if young ladies were truthfully labelled when they went into society, it would be a charming fashion, and save a world of trouble? Something in this style:—'Arabella Marabout, aged nineteen, fortune $100,000, temper warranted'; 'Laura Eau-de-Cologne, aged twenty-eight, fortune $30,000, temper slightly damaged'; Deborah Wilder, aged eighteen, fortune, one pair of hands, one head, indifferently well filled, one heart, (not in the market,) temper decided, and no expectations.' There, you see, that would do away with much of the humbug you lament, and we poor souls would know at once whether we were sought for our fortunes or ourselves, and that would be so comfortable!"

Mr. Leavenworth turned away, with a convicted sort of expression, as she spoke, and, making a spyglass of his hand, seemed to be watching something out at sea with absorbing interest. He had been guilty of a strong desire to discover whether Debby was an heiress, but had not expected to be so entirely satisfied on that important subject, and was dimly conscious that a keen eye had seen his anxiety, and a quick wit devised a means of setting it at rest forever. Somewhat disconcerted, he suddenly changed the conversation, and, like many another distressed creature, took to the water, saying briskly, —

"By-the-by, Miss Wilder, as I've engaged to do the honors, shall I have the pleasure of bathing with you when the fun begins? As you are fond of hay-making, I suppose you intend to pay your respects to the old gentleman with the three-pronged pitchfork?"

"Yes, Aunt Pen means to put me through a course of salt water, and any instructions in the art of navigation will be gratefully received; for I never saw the ocean before, and labor under a firm conviction, that, once in, I never shall come out again till I am brought, like Mr. Mantilini, a 'damp, moist, unpleasant body.'"

As Debby spoke, Mrs. Carroll hove in sight, coming down before the wind with all sails set, and signals of distress visible long before she dropped anchor and came along-side. The devoted woman had been strolling slowly for the girl's sake, though oppressed with a mournful certainty that her most prominent feature was fast becoming a fine copper-color; yet she had sustained herself like a Spartan matron, till it suddenly occurred to her that her charge might be suffering a like

> "sea-change
> Into something rich and strange."

Her fears, however, were groundless, for Debby met her without a freckle, looking all the better for her walk; and though her feet were wet with chasing the waves, and her pretty gown the worse for salt water, Aunt Pen never chid her for the destruction of her raiment, nor uttered a warning word against an unladylike exuberance of spirits, but replied to her inquiry most graciously, —

"Certainly, my love, we shall bathe at eleven, and there will be just

53

time to get Victorine and our dresses; so run on to the house, and I will join you as soon as I have finished what I am saying to Mrs. Earl,"—then added, in a stage-aside, as she put a fallen lock off the girl's forehead, "You are doing beautifully! He is evidently struck; make yourself interesting, and don't burn your nose, I beg of you."

Debby's bright face clouded over, and she walked on with so much stateliness that her escort wondered "what the deuse the old lady had done to her," and exerted himself to the utmost to recall her merry mood, but with indifferent success.

"Now I begin to feel more like myself, for this is getting back to first principles, though I fancy I look like the little old woman who fell asleep on the king's highway and woke up with abbreviated drapery; and you look funnier still, Aunt Pen," said Debby, as she tied on her pagoda-hat, and followed Mrs. Carroll, who walked out of her dressing-room an animated bale of blue cloth surmounted by a gigantic sun-bonnet.

Mr. Leavenworth was in waiting, and so like a blond-headed lobster in his scarlet suit that Debby could hardly keep her countenance as they joined the groups of bathers gathering along the breezy shore.

For an hour each day the actors and actresses who played their different roles at the —— Hotel with such precision and success put off their masks and dared to be themselves. The ocean wrought the change, for it took old and young into its arms, and for a little while they played like children in their mother's lap. No falsehood could withstand its rough sincerity; for the waves washed paint and powder from worn faces, and left a fresh bloom there. No ailment could entirely resist its vigorous cure; for every wind brought healing on its wings, endowing many a meagre life with another year of health. No gloomy spirit could refuse to listen to its lullaby, and the spray baptized it with the subtile benediction of a cheerier mood. No rank held place there; for the democratic sea toppled down the greatest statesman in the land, and dashed over the bald pate of a millionnaire with the same white-crested wave that stranded a poor parson on the beach and filled a fierce reformer's mouth with brine. No fashion ruled, but that which is as old as Eden,—the beautiful fashion of simplicity. Belles dropped their affectations with their hoops, and ran about the shore blithe-hearted girls again. Young men forgot their vices and their follies, and were not ashamed of the real courage, strength, and skill they had tried to leave behind them with their boyish plays. Old men gathered shells with the little Cupids dancing on the sand, and were better for that innocent companionship; and young mothers never looked so beautiful as when they rocked their babies on the bosom of the sea.

Debby vaguely felt this charm, and, yielding to it, splashed and sang like any beach-bird, while Aunt Pen bobbed placidly up and down in a retired corner, and Mr. Leavenworth swam to and fro, expressing his firm belief in mermaids, sirens, and the rest of the aquatic sisterhood, whose warbling no manly ear can resist.

"Miss Wilder, you must learn to swim. I've taught quantities of young ladies, and shall be delighted to launch the 'Dora,' if you'll accept me as a pilot. Stop a bit; I'll get a life-preserver," and leaving Debby to flirt with the waves, the scarlet youth departed like a flame of fire.

A dismal shriek interrupted his pupil's play, and looking up, she saw her aunt beckoning wildly with one hand, while she was groping in the water with the other. Debby ran to her, alarmed at her tragic expression, and Mrs. Carroll, drawing the girl's face into the privacy of her big bonnet, whispered one awful word, adding, distractedly, —

"Dive for them! oh, dive for them! I shall be perfectly helpless, if they are lost!"

"I can't dive, Aunt Pen; but there is a man, let us ask him," said Debby, as a black head appeared to windward.

But Mrs. Carroll's "nerves" had received a shock, and, gathering up her dripping garments, she fled precipitately along the shore and vanished into her dressing-room.

Debby's keen sense of the ludicrous got the better of her respect, and peal after peal of laughter broke from her lips, till a splash behind her put an end to her merriment, and, turning, she found that this friend in need was her acquaintance of the day before. The gentleman seemed pausing for permission to approach, with much the appearance of a sagacious Newfoundland, wistful and wet.

"Oh, I'm very glad it's you, Sir!" was Debby's cordial greeting, as she shook a drop off the end of her nose, and nodded, smiling.

The new-comer immediately beamed upon her like an amiable Triton, saying, as they turned shoreward, —

"Our first interview opened with a laugh on my side, and our second with one on yours. I accept the fact as a good omen. Your friend seemed in trouble; allow me to atone for my past misdemeanors by offering my services now. But first let me introduce myself; and as I believe in the fitness of things, let me present you with an appropriate card"; and, stooping, the young man wrote "Frank Evan" on the hard sand at Debby's feet.

The girl liked his manner, and, entering into the spirit of the thing,

56

swept as grand a curtsy as her limited drapery would allow saying, merrily,—

"I am Debby Wilder, or Dora, as aunt prefers to call me; and instead of laughing, I ought to be four feet under water, looking for something we have lost; but I can't dive, and my distress is dreadful, as you see."

"What have you lost? I will look for it, and bring it back in spite of the kelpies, if it is a human possibility," replied Mr. Evan, pushing his wet locks out of his eyes, and regarding the ocean with a determined aspect.

Debby leaned toward him, whispering with solemn countenance,—

"It is a set of teeth, Sir."

Mr. Evan was more a man of deeds than words, therefore he disappeared at once with a mighty splash, and after repeated divings and much laughter appeared bearing the chief ornament of Mrs. Penelope Carroll's comely countenance. Debby looked very pretty and grateful as she returned her thanks, and Mr. Evan was guilty of a secret wish that all the worthy lady's features were at the bottom of the sea, that he might have the satisfaction of restoring them to her attractive niece; but curbing this unnatural desire, he bowed, saying, gravely,—

"Tell your aunt, if you please, that this little accident will remain a dead secret, so far as I am concerned, and I am very glad to have been of service at such a critical moment."

Whereupon Mr. Evan marched again into the briny deep, and Debby trotted away to her aunt, whom she found a clammy heap of blue flannel and despair. Mrs. Carroll's temper was ruffled, and

57

though she joyfully rattled in her teeth, she said, somewhat testily, when Debby's story was done, —

"Now that man will have a sort of claim on us, and we must be civil, whoever he is. Dear! dear! I wish it had been Joe Leavenworth instead. Evan,—I don't remember any of our first families with connections of that name, and I dislike to be under obligations to a person of that sort, for there's no knowing how far he may presume; so, pray, be careful, Dora."

"I think you are very ungrateful, Aunt Pen; and if Mr. Evan should happen to be poor, it does not become me to turn up my nose at him, for I'm nothing but a make-believe myself just now. I don't wish to go down upon my knees to him, but I do intend to be as kind to him as I should to that conceited Leavenworth boy; yes, kinder even; for poor people value such things more, as I know very well."

Mrs. Carroll instantly recovered her temper, changed the subject, and privately resolved to confine her prejudices to her own bosom, as they seemed to have an aggravating effect upon the youthful person whom she had set her heart on disposing of to the best advantage.

Debby took her swimming-lesson with much success, and would have achieved her dinner with composure, if white-aproned gentlemen had not effectually taken away her appetite by whisking bills-of-fare into her hands, and awaiting her orders with a fatherly interest, which induced them to congregate mysterious dishes before her, and blandly rectify her frequent mistakes. She survived the ordeal, however, and at four p.m. went to drive with "that Leavenworth boy" in the finest turnout — — could produce. Aunt

Pen then came off guard, and with a sigh of satisfaction subsided into a peaceful doze, still murmuring, even in her sleep,—

"Propinquity, my love, propinquity works wonders."

"Aunt Pen, are you a modest woman?" asked the young crusader against established absurdities, as she came into the presence-chamber that evening ready for the hop.

"Bless the child, what does she mean?" cried Mrs. Carroll, with a start that twitched her back-hair out of Victorine's hands.

"Would you like to have a daughter of yours go to a party looking as I look?" continued her niece, spreading her airy dress, and standing very erect before her astonished relative.

"Why, of course I should, and be proud to own such a charming creature," regarding the slender white shape with much approbation,—adding, with a smile, as she met the girl's eye,—

"Ah, I see the difficulty, now; you are disturbed because there is not a bit of lace over these pretty shoulders of yours. Now don't be absurd, Dora; the dress is perfectly proper, or Madame Tiphany never would have sent it home. It is the fashion, child; and many a girl with such a figure would go twice as decolletee, and think nothing of it, I assure you."

Debby shook her head with an energy that set the pink heather-bells a-tremble in her hair, and her color deepened beautifully as she said, with reproachful eyes,—

"Aunt Pen, I think there is a better fashion in every young girl's heart than any Madame Tiphany can teach. I am very grateful for all you have done for me, but I cannot go into public in such an undress as this; my mother would never allow it, and father never

59

forgive it. Please don't ask me to, for indeed I cannot do it even for you."

Debby looked so pathetic that both mistress and maid broke into a laugh which somewhat reassured the young lady, who allowed her determined features to relax into a smile, as she said,—

"Now, Aunt Pen, you want me to look pretty and be a credit to you; but how would you like to see my face the color of those geraniums all the evening?"

"Why, Dora, you are out of your mind to ask such a thing, when you know it's the desire of my life to keep your color down and make you look more delicate," said her aunt, alarmed at the fearful prospect of a peony-faced protegee.

"Well, I should be anything but that, if I wore this gown in its present waistless condition; so here is a remedy which will prevent such a calamity and ease my mind."

As she spoke, Debby tied on her little blonde fichu with a gesture which left nothing more to be said.

Victorine scolded, and clasped her hands; but Mrs. Carroll, fearing to push her authority too far, made a virtue of necessity, saying, resignedly,—

"Have your own way, Dora, but in return oblige me by being agreeable to such persons as I may introduce to you; and some day, when I ask a favor, remember how much I hope to do for you, and grant it cheerfully."

"Indeed I will, Aunt Pen, if it is anything I can do without disobeying mother's 'notions' as you call them. Ask me to wear an orange-colored gown, or dance with the plainest, poorest man in the room, and I'll do it; for there never was a kinder aunt than mine in all the world," cried Debby, eager to atone for her seeming wilfulness, and really grateful for her escape from what seemed to her benighted mind a very imminent peril.

Like a clover-blossom in a vase of camellias little Debby looked that night among the dashing or languid women who surrounded her; for she possessed the charm they had lost,—the freshness of her youth. Innocent gayety sat smiling in her eyes, healthful roses bloomed upon her cheek, and maiden modesty crowned her like a garland. She was the creature that she seemed, and, yielding to the influence of the hour, danced to the music of her own blithe heart. Many felt the spell whose secret they had lost the power to divine, and watched the girlish figure as if it were a symbol of their early aspirations dawning freshly from the dimness of their past. More than one old man thought again of some little maid whose love made his boyish days a pleasant memory to him now. More than one smiling fop felt the emptiness of his smooth speech, when the truthful eyes looked up into his own; and more than one pale woman sighed regretfully with herself, "I, too, was a happy-hearted creature once!"

"That Mr. Evan does not seem very anxious to claim our acquaintance, after all, and I think better of him on that account. Has he spoken to you to-night, Dora?" asked Mrs. Carroll, as Debby dropped down beside her after a "splendid polka."

"No, ma'am, he only bowed. You see some people are not so presuming as other people thought they were; for we are not the most attractive beings on the planet; therefore a gentleman can be polite and then forget us without breaking any of the Ten Commandments. Don't be offended with him yet, for he may prove to be some great creature with a finer pedigree than any of your first families.' Mr. Leavenworth, as you know everybody, perhaps you can relieve Aunt Pen's mind, by telling her something about the tall, brown man standing behind the lady with salmon-colored hair."

Mr. Joe, who was fanning the top of Debby's head with the best intentions in life, took a survey, and answered readily, —

"Why, that's Frank Evan. I know him, and a deused good fellow he is, — though he don't belong to our set, you know."

"Indeed! pray, tell us something about him, Mr. Leavenworth. We met in the cars, and he did us a favor or two. Who and what is the man?" asked Mrs. Carroll, relenting at once toward a person who was favorably spoken of by one who did belong to her "set."

"Well, let me see," began Mr. Joe, whose narrative powers were not great. "He is a bookkeeper in my Uncle Josh Loring's importing concern, and a powerful smart man, they say. There's some kind of clever story about his father's leaving a load of debts, and Frank's working a deused number of years till they were paid. Good of him, wasn't it? Then, just as he was going to take things easier and enjoy life a bit, his mother died, and that rather knocked him up, you see. He fell sick, and came to grief generally, Uncle Josh said; so he was ordered off to get righted, and here he is, looking like a tombstone. I've a regard for Frank, for he took care of me through the smallpox a year ago, and I don't forget things of that sort; so, if you wish to be introduced, Mrs. Carroll, I'll trot him out with pleasure, and make a proud man of him."

Mrs. Carroll glanced at Debby, and as that young lady was regarding Mr. Joe with a friendly aspect, owing to the warmth of his words, she graciously assented, and the youth departed on his errand. Mr. Evan went through the ceremony with a calmness wonderful to behold, considering the position of one lady and the charms of the other, and soon glided into the conversation with the ease of a most accomplished courtier.

"Now I must tear myself away, for I'm engaged to that stout Miss Bandoline for this dance. She's a friend of my sister's, and I must do the civil, you know; powerful slow work it is, too, but I pity the poor soul,—upon my life, I do;" and Mr. Joe assumed the air of a martyr.

Debby looked up with a wicked smile in her eyes, as she said,—

"Ah, that sounds very amiable here; but in five minutes you'll be murmuring in Miss Bandoline's earm—'I've been pining to come to you this half hour, but I was obliged to take out that Miss Wilder, you see—countrified little thing enough, but not bad-looking, and has a rich aunt; so I've done my duty to her, but deuse take me if I can stand it any longer."

Mr. Evan joined in Debby's merriment; but Mr. Joe was so appalled at the sudden attack that he could only stammer a remonstrance and beat a hasty retreat, wondering how on earth she came to know that his favorite style of making himself agreeable to one young lady was by decrying another.

"Dora, my love, that is very rude, and 'Deuse' is not a proper expression for a woman's lips. Pray, restrain your lively tongue, for strangers may not understand that it is nothing but the sprightliness of your disposition which sometimes runs away with you."

"It was only a quotation, and I thought you would admire anything Mr. Leavenworth said, Aunt Pen," replied Debby, demurely.

Mrs. Carroll trod on her foot, and abruptly changed the conversation, by saying, with an appearance of deep interest, —

"Mr. Evan, you are doubtless connected with the Malcoms of Georgia; for they, I believe, are descended from the ancient Evans of Scotland. They are a very wealthy and aristocratic family, and I remember seeing their coat-of-arms once: three bannocks and a thistle."

Mr. Evan had been standing before them with a composure which impressed Mrs. Carroll with a belief in his gentle blood, for she remembered her own fussy, plebeian husband, whose fortune had never been able to purchase him the manners of a gentleman. Mr. Evan only grew a little more erect, as he replied, with an untroubled mien, —

"I cannot claim relationship with the Malcoms of Georgia or the Evans of Scotland, I believe, Madam. My father was a farmer, my grandfather a blacksmith, and beyond that my ancestors may have been street-sweepers, for anything I know; but whatever they were, I fancy they were honest men, for that has always been our boast, though, like President Jackson's, our coat-of-arms is nothing but 'a pair of shirt-sleeves.'"

From Debby's eyes there shot a bright glance of admiration for the young man who could look two comely women in the face and serenely own that he was poor. Mrs. Carroll tried to appear at ease, and, gliding out of personalities, expatiated on the comfort of "living in a land where fame and fortune were attainable by all who chose to earn them," and the contempt she felt for those "who had no sympathy with the humbler classes, no interest in the welfare of the race," and many more moral reflections as new and original as the Multiplication-Table or the Westminster Catechism. To all of

64

which Mr. Evan listened with polite deference, though there was something in the keen intelligence of his eye that made Debby blush for shallow Aunt Pen, and rejoice when the good lady got out of her depth and seized upon a new subject as a drowning mariner would a hen-coop.

"Dora, Mr. Ellenborough is coming this way; you have danced with him but once, and he is a very desirable partner; so, pray, accept, if he asks you," said Mrs. Carroll, watching a far-off individual who seemed steering his zigzag course toward them.

"I never intend to dance with Mr. Ellenborough again, so please don't urge me, Aunt Pen;" and Debby knit her brows with a somewhat irate expression.

"My love, you astonish me! He is a most agreeable and accomplished young man,—spent three years in Paris, moves in the first circles, and is considered an ornament to fashionable society.

"What can be your objection, Dora?" cried Mrs. Carroll, looking as alarmed as if her niece had suddenly announced her belief in the Koran.

"One of his accomplishments consists in drinking champagne till he is not a 'desirable partner' for any young lady with a prejudice in favor of decency. His moving in 'circles' is just what I complain of; and if he is an ornament, I prefer my society undecorated. Aunt Pen, I cannot make the nice distinctions you would have me, and a sot in broadcloth is as odious as one in rags. Forgive me, but I cannot dance with that silver-labelled decanter again."

Debby was a genuine little piece of womanhood; and though she tried to speak lightly, her color deepened, as she remembered looks that had wounded her like insults, and her indignant eyes silenced the excuses rising to her aunt's lips. Mrs. Carroll began to rue the hour she ever undertook the guidance of Sister Deborah's headstrong child, and for an instant heartily wished she had left her to bloom unseen in the shadow of the parsonage; but she concealed her annoyance, still hoping to overcome the girl's absurd resolve, by saying, mildly,—

"As you please, dear; but if you refuse Mr. Ellenborough, you will be obliged to sit through the dance, which is your favorite, you know."

Debby's countenance fell, for she had forgotten that, and the Lancers was to her the crowning rapture of the night. She paused a moment, and Aunt Pen brightened; but Debby made her little sacrifice to principle as heroically as many a greater one had been made, and, with a wistful look down the long room, answered steadily, though her foot kept time to the first strains as she spoke,—

"Then I will sit, Aunt Pen; for that is preferable to staggering about the room with a partner who has no idea of the laws of gravitation."

"Shall I have the honor of averting either calamity?" said Mr. Evan, coming to the rescue with a devotion beautiful to see; for dancing was nearly a lost art with him, and the Lancers to a novice is equal to a second Labyrinth of Crete.

"Oh, thank you!" cried Debby, tumbling fan, bouquet, and handkerchief into Mrs. Carroll's lap, with a look of relief that repaid him fourfold for the trials he was about to undergo. They went merrily away together, leaving Aunt Pen to wish that it was according to the laws of etiquette to rap officious gentlemen over the knuckles, when they introduce their fingers into private pies without permission from the chief cook. How the dance went Debby hardly knew, for the conversation fell upon books, and in the interest of her favorite theme she found even the "grand square" an impertinent interruption, while her own deficiences became almost as great as her partner's; yet, when the music ended with a flourish, and her last curtsy was successfully achieved, she longed to begin all over again, and secretly regretted that she was engaged four deep.

"How do you like our new acquaintance, Dora?" asked Aunt Pen, following Joe Leavenworth with her eye, as the "yellow-haired laddie" whirled by with the ponderous Miss Flora.

"Very much; and I'm glad we met as we did, for it makes things free and easy, and that is so agreeable in this ceremonious place," replied Debby, looking in quite an opposite direction.

"Well, I'm delighted to hear you say so, dear, for I was afraid you had taken a dislike to him, and he is really a very charming young man, just the sort of person to make a pleasant companion for a few weeks. These little friendships are part of the summer's amusement, and do no harm; so smile away. Dora, and enjoy yourself while you may."

"Yes, Aunt, I certainly will, and all the more because I have found a sensible soul to talk to. Do you know, he is very witty and well informed, though he says he never had much time for self-cultivation? But I think trouble makes people wise, and he seems to have had a good deal, though he leaves it for others to tell of. I am glad you are willing I should know him, for I shall enjoy talking about my pet heroes with him as a relief from the silly chatter I must keep up most of the time."

Mrs. Carroll was a woman of one idea; and though a slightly puzzled expression appeared in her face, she listened approvingly, and answered, with a gracious smile,—

"Of course, I should not object to your knowing such a person, my love; but I'd no idea Joe Leavenworth was a literary man, or had known much trouble, except his father's death and his sister Clementina's runaway-marriage with her drawing-master."

Debby opened her brown eyes very wide, and hastily picked at the down on her fan, but had no time to correct her aunt's mistake, for the real subject of her commendations appeared at that moment, and Mrs. Caroll was immediately absorbed in the consumption of a large pink ice.

"That girl is what I call a surprise-party, now," remarked Mr. Joe confidentially to his cigar, as he pulled off his coat and stuck his feet up in the privacy of his own apartment. "She looks as mild as strawberries and cream till you come to the complimentary, then she turns on a fellow with that deused satirical look of hers, and makes him feel like a fool. I'll try the moral dodge to-morrow and see what effect that will have; for she is mighty taking, and I must amuse myself somehow, you know."

"How many years will it take to change that fresh-hearted little girl into a fashionable belle, I wonder?" thought Frank Evan, as he climbed the four flights that led to his "sky-parlor."

"What a curious world this is!" mused Debby, with her nightcap in her hand. "The right seems odd and rude, the wrong respectable and easy, and this sort of life a merry-go-round, with no higher aim than pleasure. Well, I have made my Declaration of Independence, and Aunt Pen must be ready for a Revolution if she taxes me too heavily."

As she leaned her hot cheek on her arm, Debby's eye fell on the quaint little cap made by the motherly hands that never were tired of working for her. She touched it tenderly, and love's simple magic swept the gathering shadows from her face, and left it clear again, as her thoughts flew home like birds into the shelter of their nest.

"Good night, mother! I'll face temptation steadily. I'll try to take life cheerily, and do nothing that shall make your dear face a reproach, when it looks into my own again."

Then Debby said her prayers like any pious child, and lay down to dream of pulling buttercups with Baby Bess, and singing in the twilight on her father's knee.

The history of Debby's first day might serve as a sample of most that followed, as week after week went by with varying pleasures and increasing interest to more than one young debutante.

Mrs. Carroll did her best, but Debby was too simple for a belle, too honest for a flirt, too independent for a fine lady; she would be nothing but her sturdy little self, open as daylight, gay as a lark, and blunt as any Puritan. Poor Aunt Pen was in despair, till she observed that the girl often "took" with the very peculiarities which she was lamenting; this somewhat consoled her, and she tried to make the best of the pretty bit of homespun which would not and could not become velvet or brocade. Seguin, Ellenborough, & Co. looked with lordly scorn upon her, as a worm blind to their attractions. Miss MacRimsy and her "set" quizzed her unmercifully behind her back, after being worsted in several passages of arms; and more than one successful mamma condoled with Aunt Pen upon the terribly defective education of her charge, till that stout matron could have found it in her heart to tweak off their caps and walk on them, like the irascible Betsey Trotwood.

But Debby had a circle of admirers who loved her with a sincerity few summer queens could boast; for they were real friends, won by gentle arts, and retained by the gracious sweetness of her nature. Moon-faced babies crowed and clapped their chubby hands when she passed by their wicker-thrones; story-loving children clustered round her knee, and never were denied; pale invalids found wild-flowers on their pillows; and forlorn papas forgot the state of the moneymarket when she sang for them the homely airs their daughters had no time to learn. Certain plain young ladies poured their woes into her friendly ear, and were comforted; several smart Sophomores fell into a state of chronic stammer, blush, and adoration, when she took a motherly interest in their affairs; and a melancholy old Frenchman blessed her with the enthusiasm of his nation, because she put a posy in the button-hole of his rusty coat, and never failed to smile and bow as he passed by. Yet Debby was no Edgworth heroine preternaturally prudent, wise, and untemptable; she had a fine crop of piques, vanities, and dislikes growing up under this new style of cultivation. She loved admiration, enjoyed her purple and fine linen, hid new-born envy, disappointed hope, and wounded pride behind a smiling face, and often thought with a sigh of the humdrum duties that awaited her at home. But under the airs and graces Aunt Pen cherished with such sedulous care, under the flounces and furbelows Victorine daily adjusted with groans, under the polish which she acquired with feminine ease, the girl's heart still beat steadfast and strong, and conscience kept watch and ward that no traitor should enter in to surprise the citadel which mother-love had tried to garrison so well.

In pursuance of his sage resolve, Mr. Joe tried the "moral dodge," as he elegantly expressed it, and, failing in that, followed it up with the tragic, religious, negligent, and devoted ditto; but acting was not his forte, so Debby routed him in all; and at last, when he was at his wit's end for an idea, she suggested one, and completed her victory by saying pleasantly, —

"You took me behind the curtain too soon, and now the paste-diamonds and cotton-velvet don't impose upon me a bit. Just be your natural self, and we shall get on nicely, Mr. Leavenworth."

The novelty of the proposal struck his fancy, and after a few relapses it was carried into effect and thenceforth, with Debby, he became the simple, good-humored lad Nature designed him to be, and, as a proof of it, soon fell very sincerely in love.

Frank Evan, seated in the parquet of society, surveyed the dress-circle with much the same expression that Debby had seen during Aunt Pen's oration; but he soon neglected that amusement to watch several actors in the drama going on before his eyes, while a strong desire to perform a part therein slowly took possession of his mind.

Debby always had a look of welcome when he came, always treated him with the kindness of a generous woman who has had an opportunity to forgive, and always watched the serious, solitary man with a great compassion for his loss, a growing admiration for his upright life. More than once the beach-birds saw two figures pacing the sands at sunrise with the peace of early day upon their faces and the light of a kindred mood shining in their eyes. More than once the friendly ocean made a third in the pleasant conversation, and its low undertone came and went between the mellow bass and silvery treble of the human voices with a melody that lent another charm to interviews which soon grew wondrous sweet to man and maid. Aunt Pen seldom saw the twain together, seldom spoke of Evan; and Debby held her peace, for, when she planned to make her innocent confessions, she found that what

71

seemed much to her was nothing to another ear and scarcely worth the telling; so, unconscious as yet whither the green path led, she went on her way, leading two lives, one rich and earnest, hoarded deep within herself, the other frivolous and gay for all the world to criticize. But those venerable spinsters, the Fates, took the matter into their own hands, and soon got the better of those short-sighted matrons, Mesdames Grundy and Carroll; for, long before they knew it, Frank and Debby had begun to read together a book greater than Dickens ever wrote, and when they had come to the fairest part of the sweet story Adam first told Eve, they looked for the name upon the title-page, and found that it was "Love."

Fight weeks came and went,—eight wonderfully happy weeks to Debby and her friend; for "propinquity" had worked more wonders than poor Mrs. Carroll knew, as the only one she saw or guessed was the utter captivation of Joe Leavenworth. He had become "himself" to such an extent that a change of identity would have been a relief; for the object of his adoration showed no signs of relenting, and he began to fear, that, as Debby said, her heart was "not in the market." She was always friendly, but never made those interesting betrayals of regard which are so encouraging to youthful gentlemen "who fain would climb, yet fear to fall." She never blushed when he pressed her hand, never fainted or grew pale when he appeared with a smashed trotting-wagon and black eye, and actually slept through a serenade that would have won any other woman's soul out of her body with its despairing quavers. Matters were getting desperate; for horses lost their charms, "flowing bowls" palled upon his lips, ruffled shirt-bosoms no longer delighted him, and hops possessed no soothing power to allay the anguish of his mind. Mr. Seguin, after unavailing ridicule and pity, took compassion on him, and from his large experience suggested a remedy, just as he was departing for a more congenial sphere.

"Now don't be an idiot, Joe, but, if you want to keep your hand in and go through a regular chapter of flirtation, just right about face, and devote yourself to some one else. Nothing like jealousy to teach womankind their own minds, and a touch of it will bring little Wilder round in a jiffy. Try it, my boy, and good luck to you!" — with which Christian advice Mr. Seguin slapped his pupil on the shoulder, and disappeared, like a modern Mephistopheles, in a cloud of cigar-smoke.

"I'm glad he's gone, for in my present state of mind he's not up to my mark at all. I'll try his plan, though, and flirt with Clara West; she's engaged, so it won't damage her affections; her lover isn't here, so it won't disturb his; and, by Jove! I must do something, for I can't stand this suspense."

Debby was infinitely relieved by this new move, and infinitely amused as she guessed the motive that prompted it; but the more contented she seemed, the more violently Mr. Joe flirted with her rival, till at last weak-minded Miss Clara began to think her absent George the most undesirable of lovers, and to mourn that she ever said "Yes" to a merchant's clerk, when she might have said it to a merchant's son. Aunt Pen watched and approved this stratagem, hoped for the best results, and believed the day won when Debby grew pale and silent, and followed with her eyes the young couple who were playing battledore and shuttle-cock with each other's hearts, as if she took some interest in the game. But Aunt Pen clashed her cymbals too soon; for Debby's trouble had a better source than jealousy, and in the silence of the sleepless nights that stole her bloom she was taking counsel of her own full heart, and resolving to serve another woman as she would herself be served in

73

a like peril, though etiquette was outraged and the customs of polite society turned upside down.

"Look, Aunt Pen! what lovely shells and moss I've got! Such a splendid scramble over the rocks as I've had with Mrs. Duncan's boys! It seemed so like home to run and sing with a troop of topsy-turvy children that it did me good; and I wish you had all been there to see." cried Debby, running into the drawing-room, one day, where Mrs. Carroll and a circle of ladies sat enjoying a dish of highly flavored scandal, as they exercised their eyesight over fancy-work.

"My dear Dora, spare my nerves; and if you have any regard for the proprieties of life, don't go romping in the sun with a parcel of noisy boys. If you could see what an object you are, I think you would try to imitate Miss Clara, who is always a model of elegant repose."

Miss West primmed up her lips, and settled a fold in her ninth flounce, as Mrs. Carroll spoke, while the whole group fixed their eyes with dignified disapproval on the invader of their refined society. Debby had come like a fresh wind into a sultry room; but no one welcomed the healthful visitant, no one saw a pleasant picture in the bright-faced girl with windtossed hair and rustic hat heaped with moss and many-tinted shells; they only saw that her gown was wet, her gloves forgotten, and her scarf trailing at her waist in a manner no well-bred lady could approve. The sunshine faded out of Debby's face, and there was a touch of bitterness in her tone, as she glanced at the circle of fashion-plates, saying with an earnestness which caused Miss West to open her pale eyes to their widest extent, —

"Aunt Pen, don't freeze me yet, — don't take away my faith in simple things, but let me be a child a little longer,—let me play and sing and keep my spirit blithe among the dandelions and the robins while I can; for trouble comes soon enough, and all my life will be the richer and the better for a happy youth."

Mrs. Carroll had nothing at hand to offer in reply to this appeal, and four ladies dropped their work to stare; but Frank Evan looked in from the piazza, saying, as he beckoned like a boy,—

"I'll play with you, Miss Dora; come and make sand pies upon the shore. Please let her, Mrs. Carroll; we'll be very good, and not wet our pinafores or feet."

Without waiting for permission, Debby poured her treasures into the lap of a certain lame Freddy, and went away to a kind of play she had never known before. Quiet as a chidden child, she walked beside her companion, who looked down at the little figure, longing to take it on his knee and call the sunshine back again. That he dared not do; but accident, the lover's friend, performed the work, and did him a good turn beside. The old Frenchman was slowly approaching, when a frolicsome wind whisked off his hat and sent it skimming along the beach. In spite of her late lecture, away went Debby, and caught the truant chapeau just as a wave was hurrying up to claim it. This restored her cheerfulness, and when she returned, she was herself again.

"A thousand thanks; but does Mademoiselle remember the forfeit I might demand to add to the favor she has already done me?" asked the gallant old gentleman, as Debby took the hat off her own head, and presented it with a martial salute.

"Ah, I had forgotten that; but you may claim [text missing in original copy] do something more to give you pleasure;" and Debby

75

looked up into the withered face which had grown familiar to her, with kind eyes, full of pity and respect.

Her manner touched the old man very much; he bent his gray head before her, saying, gratefully,—

"My child, I am not good enough to salute these blooming checks; but I shall pray the Virgin to reward you for the compassion you bestow on the poor exile, and I shall keep your memory very green through all my life."

He kissed her hand, as if it were a queen's, and went on his way, thinking of the little daughter whose death left him childless in a foreign land.

Debby softly began to sing, "Oh, come unto the yellow sands!" but stopped in the middle of a line, to say,—

"Shall I tell you why I did what Aunt Pen would call a very unladylike and improper thing, Mr. Evans?"

"If you will be so kind;" and her companion looked delighted at the confidence about to be reposed in him.

"Somewhere across this great wide sea I hope I have a brother," Debby said, with softened voice and a wistful look into the dim horizon. "Five years ago he left us, and we have never heard from him since, except to know that he landed safely in Australia. People tell us he is dead; but I believe he will yet come home; and so I love to help and pity any man who needs it, rich or poor, young or old, hoping that as I do by them some tender-hearted woman far away will do by Brother Will."

As Debby spoke, across Frank Evan's face there passed the look that seldom comes but once to any young man's countenance; for

76

suddenly the moment dawned when love asserted its supremacy, and putting pride, doubt, and fear underneath its feet, ruled the strong heart royally and bent it to its will. Debby's thoughts had floated across the sea; but they came swiftly back when her companion spoke again, steadily and slow, but with a subtile change in tone and manner which arrested them at once.

"Miss Dora, if you should meet a man who had known a laborious youth, a solitary manhood, who had no sweet domestic ties to make home beautiful and keep his nature warm, who longed most ardently to be so blessed, and made it the aim of his life to grow more worthy the good gift, should it ever come,—if you should learn that you possessed the power to make this fellow-creature's happiness, could you find it in your gentle heart to take compassion on him for the love of 'Brother Will'?"

Debby was silent, wondering why heart and nerves and brain were stirred by such a sudden thrill, why she dared not look up, and why, when she desired so much to speak, she could only answer, in a voice that sounded strange to her own ears,—

"I cannot tell."

Still, steadily and slow, with strong emotion deepening and softening his voice, the lover at her side went on,—

"Will you ask yourself this question in some quiet hour? For such a man has lived in the sunshine of your presence for eight happy weeks, and now, when his holiday is done, he finds that the old solitude will be more sorrowful than ever, unless he can discover whether his summer dream will change into a beautiful reality. Miss Dora, I have very little to offer you; a faithful heart to cherish you, a strong arm to work for you, an honest name to give into your

77

keeping,—these are all; but if they have any worth in your eyes, they are most truly yours forever."

Debby was steadying her voice to reply, when a troop of bathers came shouting down the bank, and she took flight into her dressing-room, there to sit staring at the wall, till the advent of Aunt Pen forced her to resume the business of the hour by assuming her aquatic attire and stealing shyly down into the surf.

Frank Evan, still pacing in the footprints they had lately made, watched the lithe figure tripping to and fro, and, as he looked, murmured to himself the last line of a ballad Debby sometimes sang,—

"Dance light! for my heart it lies under your feet, love!"

Presently a great wave swept Debby up, and stranded her very near him, much to her confusion and his satisfaction. Shaking the spray out of her eyes, she was hurrying away, when Frank said,—

"You will trip, Miss Dora; let me tie these strings for you;" and, suiting the action to the word, he knelt down and began to fasten the cords of her bathing shoe.

Debby stood Looking down at the tall head bent before her, with a curious sense of wonder that a look from her could make a strong man flush and pale, as he had done; and she was trying to concoct some friendly speech, when Frank, still fumbling at the knots, said, very earnestly and low,—

"Forgive me, if I am selfish in pressing for an answer; but I must go to-morrow, and a single word will change my whole future for the better or the worse. Won't you speak it, Dora?"

If they had been alone, Debby would have put her arms about his
78

neck, and said it with all her heart; but she had a presentiment that she should cry, if her love found vent; and here forty pairs of eyes were on them, and salt water seemed superfluous. Besides, Debby had not breathed the air of coquetry so long without a touch of the infection; and the love of power, that lies dormant in the meekest woman's breast, suddenly awoke and tempted her.

"If you catch me before I reach that rock, perhaps I will say 'Yes,'" was her unexpected answer; and before her lover caught her meaning, she was floating leisurely away.

Frank was not in bathing-costume, and Debby never dreamed that he would take her at her word; but she did not know the man she had to deal with; for, taking no second thought, he flung hat and coat away, and dashed into the sea. This gave a serious aspect to Debby's foolish jest. A feeling of dismay seized her, when she saw a resolute face dividing the waves behind her, and thought of the rash challenge she had given; but she had a spirit of her own, and had profited well by Mr. Joe's instructions: so she drew a long breath, and swam as if for life, instead of love. Evan was incumbered by his clothing, and Debby had much the start of him; but, like a second Leander, he hoped to win his Hero, and, lending every muscle to the work, gained rapidly upon the little hat which was his beacon through the foam. Debby heard the deep breathing drawing nearer and nearer, as her pursuer's strong arms cleft the water and sent it rippling past her lips, something like terror took possession of her; for the strength seemed going out of her limbs, and the rock appeared to recede before her; but the unconquerable blood of the Pilgrims was in her veins, and "Nil desperandum" her motto; so, setting her teeth, she muttered, defiantly, —

"I'll not be beaten, if I go to the bottom!"

A great splashing arose, and when Evan recovered the use of his eyes, the pagoda-hat had taken a sudden turn, and seemed making for the farthest point of the goal. "I am sure of her now," thought Frank; and, like a gallant seagod, he bore down upon his prize, clutching it with a shout of triumph. But the hat was empty, and like a mocking echo came Debby's laugh, as she climbed, exhausted, to a cranny in the rock.

"A very neat thing, by Jove! Deuse take me if you a'n't 'an honor to your teacher, and a terror to the foe,' Miss Wilder," cried Mr. Joe, as he came up from a solitary cruise and dropped anchor at her side. "Here, bring along the hat, Evan; I'm going to crown the victor with appropriate what-d'ye-call-'ems," he continued, pulling a handful of sea-weed that looked like well-boiled greens.

Frank came up, smiling; but his lips were white, and in his eye a look Debby could not meet; so, being full of remorse, she naturally assumed an air of gayety, and began to sing the merriest air she knew, merely because she longed to throw herself upon the stones and cry violently.

"It was 'most as exciting as a regatta, and you pulled well, Evan; but you had too much ballast aboard, and Miss Wilder ran up false colors just in time to save her ship. What was the wager?" asked the lively Joseph, complacently surveying his marine millinery, which would have scandalized a fashionable mermaid.

"Only a trifle," answered Debby, knotting up her braids with a revengeful jerk.

"It's taken the wind out of your sails, I fancy, Evan, for you look immensely Byronic with the starch minus in your collar and your hair in a poetic toss. Come, I'll try a race with you; and Miss Wilder

80

will dance all the evening with the winner. Bless the man, what's he doing down there? Burying sunfish, hey?"

Frank had been sitting below them on a narrow strip of sand, absently piling up a little mound that bore some likeness to a grave. As his companion spoke, he looked at it, and a sudden flush of feeling swept across his face, as he replied, —

"No, only a dead hope."

"Deuse take it, yes, a good many of that sort of craft founder in these waters, as I know to my sorrow;" and, sighing tragically. Mr. Joe turned to help Debby from her perch, but she had glided silently into the sea, and was gone.

For the next four hours the poor girl suffered the sharpest pain she had ever known; for now she clearly saw the strait her folly had betrayed her into. Frank Evan was a proud man, and would not ask her love again, believing she had tacitly refused it; and how could she tell him that she had trifled with the heart she wholly loved and longed to make her own? She could not confide in Aunt Pen, for that worldly lady would have no sympathy to bestow. She longed for her mother; but there was no time to write, for Frank was going on the morrow, — might even then be gone; and as this fear came over her, she covered up her face and wished that she were dead. Poor Debby! her last mistake was sadder than her first, and she was reaping a bitter harvest from her summer's sowing. She sat and thought till her cheeks burned and her temples throbbed; but she dared not ease her pain with tears. The gong sounded like a Judgment-Day trump of doom, and she trembled at the idea of confronting many eyes with such a telltale face; but she could not stay behind, for Aunt Pen must know the cause. She tried to play her hard part well; but wherever she looked, some fresh anxiety appeared, as if every fault and folly of those months had blossomed suddenly within the hour. She saw Frank Evan more sombre and more solitary than when she met him first, and cried regretfully within herself, "How could I so forget the truth I owed him?"—She saw Clara West watching with eager eyes for the coming of young Leavenworth, and sighed,—"This is the fruit of my wicked vanity!" She saw Aunt Pen regarded her with an anxious face, and longed to say, "Forgive me, for I have not been sincere!" At last, as her trouble grew, she resolved to go away and have a quiet "think,"—a remedy which had served her in many a lesser perplexity; so, stealing out, she went to a grove of cedars usually deserted at that hour. But in ten minutes Joe Leavenworth appeared at the door of the summer house, and, looking in, said, with a well-acted start of pleasure and surprise,—

"Beg pardon, I thought there was no one here, My dear Miss Wilder, you look contemplative; but I fancy it wouldn't do to ask the subject of your meditations, would it?"

He paused with such an evident intention of remaining that Debby resolved to make use of the moment, and ease her conscience of one care that burdened it; therefore she answered his question with her usual directness,—

"My meditations were partly about you."

Mr. Joe was guilty of the weakness of blushing violently and looking immensely gratified; but his rapture was of short duration, for Debby went on very earnestly,—

"I believe I am going to do what you may consider a very impertinent thing; but I would rather be unmannerly than unjust to others or untrue to my own sense of right. Mr. Leavenworth, if you were an older man, I should not dare to say this to you; but I have brothers of my own, and, remembering how many unkind things they do for want of thought, I venture to remind you that a woman's heart is a perilous plaything, and too tender to be used for a selfish purpose or an hour's pleasure. I know this kind of amusement is not considered wrong; but it is wrong, and I cannot shut my eyes to the fact, or sit silent while another woman is allowed to deceive herself and wound the heart that trusts her. Oh, if you love your own sisters, be generous, be just, and do not destroy that poor girl's happiness, but go away before your sport becomes a bitter pain to her!"

Joe Leavenworth had stood staring at Debby with a troubled countenance, feeling as if all the misdemeanors of his life were about to be paraded before him; but, as he listened to her plea, the womanly spirit that prompted it appealed more loudly than her words, and in his really generous heart he felt regret for what had never seemed a fault before. Shallow as he was, nature was stronger than education, and he admired and accepted what many a wiser, worldlier man would have resented with anger or contempt. He loved Debby with all his little might; he meant to tell her so, and graciously present his fortune and himself for her acceptance; but now, when the moment came, the well-turned speech he had prepared vanished from his memory, and with the better eloquence of feeling he blundered out his passion like a very boy.

"Miss Dora, I never meant to make trouble between Clara and her lover; upon my soul, I didn't, and wish Seguin had not put the notion into my head, since it has given you pain. I only tried to pique you into showing some regret, when I neglected you; but you didn't, and then I got desperate and didn't care what became of any one. Oh, Dora, if you knew how much I loved you, I am sure you'd

83

forgive it, and let me prove my repentance by giving up everything that you dislike. I mean what I say; upon my life I do; and I'll keep my word, if you will only let me hope."

If Debby had wanted a proof of her love for Frank Evan, she might have found it in the fact that she had words enough at her command now, and no difficulty in being sisterly pitiful toward her second suitor.

"Please get up," she said; for Mr. Joe, feeling very humble and very earnest, had gone down upon his knees, and sat there entirely regardless of his personal appearance.

He obeyed; and Debby stood looking up at him with her kindest aspect, as she said, more tenderly than she had ever spoken to him before,—

"Thank you for the affection you offer me, but I cannot accept it, for I have nothing to give you in return but the friendliest regard, the most sincere good-will. I know you will forgive me, and do for your own sake the good things you would have done for mine, that I may add to my esteem a real respect for one who has been very kind to me."

"I'll try,—indeed, I will, Miss Dora, though it will be powerful hard without yourself for a help and a reward."

Poor Joe choked a little, but called up an unexpected manliness, and added, stoutly,—

"Don't think I shall be offended at your speaking so or saying 'No' to me,—not a bit; it's all right, and I'm much obliged to you. I might have known you couldn't care for such a fellow as I am, and don't blame you, for nobody in the world is good enough for you. I'll go

84

away at once, I'll try to keep my promise, and I hope you'll be very happy all your life."

He shook Debby's bands heartily, and hurried down the steps, but at the bottom paused and looked back. Debby stood upon the threshold with sunshine dancing on her winsome face, and kind words trembling on her lips; for the moment it seemed impossible to part, and, with an impetuous gesture, he cried to her, —

"Oh, Dora, let me stay and try to win you! for everything is possible to love, and I never knew how dear you were to me till now!"

There were sudden tears in the young man's eyes, the flush of a genuine emotion on his cheek, the tremor of an ardent longing in his voice, and, for the first time, a very true affection strengthened his whole countenance. Debby's heart was full of penitence; she had given so much pain to more than one that she longed to atone for it—longed to do some very friendly thing, and soothe some trouble such as she herself had known. She looked into the eager face uplifted to her own and thought of Will, then stooped and touched her lover's forehead with the lips that softly whispered, "No."

If she had cared for him, she never would have done it; poor Joe knew that, and murmuring an incoherent "Thank you!" he rushed away, feeling very much as he remembered to have felt when his baby sister died and he wept his grief away upon his mother's neck. He began his preparations for departure at once, in a burst of virtuous energy quite refreshing to behold, thinking within himself, as he flung his cigar-case into the grate, kicked a billiard-ball into a corner, and suppressed his favorite allusion to the Devil, —

"This is a new sort of thing to me, but I can bear it, and upon my life I think I feel the better for it already."

And so he did; for though he was no Augustine to turn in an hour from worldly hopes and climb to sainthood through long years of inward strife, yet in aftertimes no one knew how many false steps had been saved, how many small sins repented of, through the power of the memory that far away a generous woman waited to respect him, and in his secret soul he owned that one of the best moments of his life was that in which little Debby Wilder whispered "No," and kissed him.

As he passed from sight, the girl leaned her head upon her hand, thinking sorrowfully to herself,—

"What right had I to censure him, when my own actions are so far from true? I have done a wicked thing, and as an honest girl I should undo it, if I can. I have broken through the rules of a false propriety for Clara's sake; can I not do as much for Frank's? I will. I'll find him, if I search the house,—and tell him all, though I never dare to look him in the face again, and Aunt Pen sends me home to-morrow."

Full of zeal and courage, Debby caught up her hat and ran down the steps, but, as she saw Frank Evan coming up the path, a sudden panic fell upon her, and she could only stand mutely waiting his approach.

It is asserted that Love is blind; and on the strength of that popular delusion novel heroes and heroines go blundering through three volumes of despair with the plain truth directly under their absurd noses: but in real life this theory is not supported; for to a living man the countenance of a loving woman is more eloquent than any language, more trustworthy than a world of proverbs, more beautiful than the sweetest love-lay ever sung.

Frank looked at Debby, and "all her heart stood up in her eyes," as she stretched her hands to him, though her lips only whispered very low, —

"Forgive me, and let me say the 'Yes' I should have said so long ago."

Had she required any assurance of her lover's truth, or any reward for her own, she would have found it in the change that dawned so swiftly in his face, smoothing the lines upon his forehead, lighting the gloom of his eye, stirring his firm lips with a sudden tremor, and making his touch as soft as it was strong. For a moment both stood very still, while Debby's tears streamed down like summer rain; then Frank drew her into the green shadow of the grove, and its peace soothed her like a mother's voice, till she looked up smiling with a shy delight her glance had never known before. The slant sunbeams dropped a benediction on their heads, the robins peeped, and the cedars whispered, but no rumor of what further passed ever went beyond the precincts of the wood; for such hours are sacred, and Nature guards the first blossoms of a human love as tenderly as she nurses May-flowers underneath the leaves.

Mrs. Carroll had retired to her bed with a nervous headache, leaving Debby to the watch and ward of friendly Mrs. Earle, who performed her office finely by letting her charge entirely alone. In her dreams Aunt Pen was just imbibing a copious draught of champagne at the wedding-breakfast of her niece, "Mrs. Joseph Leavenworth," when she was roused by the bride elect, who passed through the room with a lamp and a shawl in her hand.

"What time is it, and where are you going, dear?" she asked, dozily wondering if the carriage for the wedding-tour was at the door so soon.

"It's only nine, and I am going for a sail, Aunt Pen."

As Debby spoke, the light flashed full into her face, and a sudden thought into Mrs. Carroll's mind. She rose up from her pillow, looking as stately in her night-cap as Maria Theresa is said to have done in like unassuming head-gear.

"Something has happened, Dora! What have you done? What have you said? I insist upon knowing immediately," she demanded, with somewhat startling brevity.

"I have said 'No' to Mr. Leavenworth and 'Yes' to Mr. Evan; and I should like to go home to-morrow, if you please," was the equally concise reply.

Mrs. Carroll fell flat in her bed, and lay there stiff and rigid as Morlena Kenwigs. Debby gently drew the curtains, and stole away leaving Aunt Pen's wrath to effervesce before morning.

The moon was hanging luminous and large on the horizon's edge, sending shafts of light before her till the melancholy ocean seemed to smile, and along that shining pathway happy Debby and her lover floated into that new world where all things seem divine.

THE BROTHERS

Doctor Franck came in as I sat sewing up the rents in an old shirt, that Tom might go tidily to his grave. New shirts were needed for the living, and there was no wife or mother to "dress him handsome when he went to meet the Lord," as one woman said, describing the fine funeral she had pinched herself to give her son.

"Miss Dane, I'm in a quandary," began the Doctor, with that expression of countenance which says as plainly as words, "I want to ask a favor, but I wish you'd save me the trouble."

"Can I help you out of it?

"Faith! I don't like to propose it, but you certainly can, if you please."

"Then give it a name, I beg."

"You see a Reb has just been brought in crazy with typhoid; a bad case every way; a drunken, rascally little captain somebody took the trouble to capture, but whom nobody wants to take the trouble to cure. The wards are full, the ladies worked to death, and willing to be for our own boys, but rather slow to risk their lives for a Reb. Now you've had the fever, you like queer patients, your mate will see to your ward for a while, and I will find you a good attendant. The fellow won't last long, I fancy; but he can't die without some sort of care, you know. I've put him in the fourth story of the west wing, away from the rest. It is airy, quiet, and comfortable there. I'm on that ward, and will do my best for you in every way. Now, then, will you go?"

"Of course I will, out of perversity, if not common charity; for some of these people think that because I'm an abolitionist I am also a heathen, and I should rather like to show them, that, though I cannot quite love my enemies, I am willing to take care of them."

"Very good; I thought you'd go; and speaking of abolition reminds me that you can have a contraband for servant, if you like. It is that fine mulatto fellow who was found burying his Rebel master after the fight, and, being badly cut over the head, our boys brought him along. Will you have him?"

"By all means,—for I'll stand to my guns on that point, as on the other; these black boys are far more faithful and handy than some of the white scamps given me to serve, instead of being served by. But is this man well enough?"

"Yes, for that sort of work, and I think you'll like him. He must have been a handsome fellow before he got his face slashed; not much darker than myself; his master's son, I dare say, and the white blood makes him rather high and haughty about some things. He was in a bad way when he came in, but vowed he'd die in the street rather than turn in with the black fellows below; so I put him up in the west wing, to be out of the way, and he's seen to the captain all the morning. When can you go up?"

"As soon as Tom is laid out, Skinner moved, Haywood washed, Marble dressed, Charley rubbed, Downs taken up, Upham laid down, and the whole forty fed."

We both laughed, though the Doctor was on his way to the deadhouse and I held a shroud on my lap. But in a hospital one learns that cheerfulness is one's salvation; for, in an atmosphere of suffering and death, heaviness of heart would soon paralyze usefulness of hand, if the blessed gift of smiles had been denied us.

In an hour I took possession of my new charge, finding a dissipated-looking boy of nineteen or twenty raving in the solitary little room, with no one near him but the contraband in the room adjoining. Feeling decidedly more interest in the black man than in the white, yet remembering the Doctor's hint of his being "high and haughty," I glanced furtively at him as I scattered chloride of lime about the room to purify the air, and settled matters to suit myself. I had seen many contrabands, but never one so attractive as this. All colored men are called "boys," even if their heads are white; this boy was five-and-twenty at least, strong-limbed and manly, and had the look of one who never had been cowed by abuse or worn with oppressive labor. He sat on his bed doing nothing; no book, no pipe, no pen or paper anywhere appeared, yet anything less indolent or listless than his attitude and expression I never saw. Erect he sat with a hand on either knee, and eyes fixed on the bare wall opposite, so rapt in some absorbing thought as to be unconscious of my presence, though the door stood wide open and my movements were by no means noiseless. His face was half averted, but I instantly approved the Doctor's taste, for the profile which I saw possessed all the attributes of comeliness belonging to his mixed race. He was more quadroon than mulatto, with Saxon features, Spanish complexion darkened by exposure, color in lips and cheek, waving hair, and an eye full of the passionate melancholy which in such men always seems to utter a mute protest against the broken law that doomed them at their birth. What could he be thinking of? The sick boy cursed and raved, I rustled to and fro, steps passed the door, bells rang, and the steady rumble of army-wagons came up from the street, still he never stirred. I had seen colored people in what they call "the black sulks," when, for days, they neither smiled nor spoke, and scarcely ate. But this was something more than that; for the man was not dully

91

brooding over some small grievance,—he seemed to see an all-absorbing fact or fancy recorded on the wall, which was a blank to me. I wondered if it were some deep wrong or sorrow, kept alive by memory and impotent regret; if he mourned for the dead master to whom he had been faithful to the end; or if the liberty now his were robbed of half its sweetness by the knowledge that some one near and dear to him still languished in the hell from which he had escaped. My heart quite warmed to him at that idea; I wanted to know and comfort him; and, following the impulse of the moment, I went in and touched him on the shoulder.

In an instant the man vanished and the slave appeared. Freedom was too new a boon to have wrought its blessed changes yet, and as he started up, with his hand at his temple and an obsequious "Yes, Ma'am," any romance that had gathered round him fled away, leaving the saddest of all sad facts in living guise before me. Not only did the manhood seem to die out of him, but the comeliness that first attracted me; for, as he turned, I saw the ghastly wound that had laid open cheek and forehead. Being partly healed, it was no longer bandaged, but held together with strips of that transparent plaster which I never see without a shiver and swift recollections of scenes with which it is associated in my mind. Part of his black hair had been shorn away, and one eye was nearly closed; pain so distorted, and the cruel sabre-cut so marred that portion of his face, that, when I saw it, I felt as if a fine medal had been suddenly reversed, showing me a far more striking type of human suffering and wrong than Michel Angelo's bronze prisoner. By one of those inexplicable processes that often teach us how little we understand ourselves, my purpose was suddenly changed, and though I went in to offer comfort as a friend, I merely gave an order as a mistress.

92

"Will you open these windows? this man needs more air."

He obeyed at once, and, as he slowly urged up the unruly sash, the handsome profile was again turned toward me, and again I was possessed by my first impression so strongly that I involuntarily said,—

"Thank you, Sir."

Perhaps it was fancy, but I thought that in the look of mingled surprise and something like reproach which he gave me there was also a trace of grateful pleasure. But he said, in that tone of spiritless humility these poor souls learn so soon,—

"I ain't a white man, Ma'am, I'm a contraband."

"Yes, I know it; but a contraband is a free man, and I heartily congratulate you."

He liked that; his face shone, he squared his shoulders, lifted his head, and looked me full in the eye with a brisk—

"Thank ye, Ma'am; anything more to do fer yer?"

"Doctor Franck thought you would help me with this man, as there are many patients and few nurses or attendants. Have you had the fever?"

"No, Ma'am."

"They should have thought of that when they put him here; wounds and fevers should not be together. I'll try to get you moved."

He laughed a sudden laugh,—if he had been a white man, I should have called it scornful; as he was a few shades darker than myself, I

93

suppose it must be considered an insolent, or at least an unmannerly one.

"It don't matter, Ma'am. I'd rather be up here with the fever than down with those niggers; and there ain't no other place fer me."

Poor fellow! that was true. No ward in all the hospital would take him in to lie side by side with the most miserable white wreck there. Like the bat in Aesop's fable, he belonged to neither race; and the pride of one, the helplessness of the other, kept him hovering alone in the twilight a great sin has brought to overshadow the whole land.

"You shall stay, then; for I would far rather have you than any lazy Jack. But are you well and strong enough?"

"I guess I'll do, Ma'am."

He spoke with a passive sort of acquiescence, — as if it did not much matter, if he were not able, and no one would particularly rejoice, if he were.

"Yes, I think you will. By what name shall I call you?"

"Bob, Ma'am."

Every woman has her pet whim; one of mine was to teach the men self-respect by treating them respectfully. Tom, Dick, and Harry would pass, when lads rejoiced in those familiar abbreviations; but to address men often old enough to be my father in that style did not suit my old-fashioned ideas of propriety. This "Bob" would never do; I should have found it as easy to call the chaplain "Gus" as my tragical-looking contraband by a title so strongly associated with the tail of a kite.

94

"What is your other name?" I asked. "I like to call my attendants by their last names rather than by their first."

"I've got no other, Ma'am; we have our masters' names, or do without. Mine's dead, and I won't have anything of his about me."

"Well, I'll call you Robert, then, and you may fill this pitcher for me, if you will be so kind."

He went; but, through all the tame, obedience years of servitude had taught him, I could see that the proud spirit his father gave him was not yet subdued, for the look and gesture with which he repudiated his master's name were a more effective declaration of independence than any Fourth-of-July orator could have prepared.

We spent a curious week together. Robert seldom left his room, except upon my errands; and I was a prisoner all day, often all night, by the bedside of the Rebel. The fever burned itself rapidly away, for there seemed little vitality to feed it in the feeble frame of this old young man, whose life had been none of the most righteous, judging from the revelations made by his unconscious lips; since more than once Robert authoritatively silenced him, when my gentler bushings were of no avail, and blasphemous wanderings or ribald camp-songs made my cheeks burn and Robert's face assume an aspect of disgust. The captain was a gentleman in the world's eye, but the contraband was the gentleman in mine;—I was a fanatic, and that accounts for such depravity of taste, I hope. I never asked Robert of himself, feeling that somewhere there was a spot still too sore to bear the lightest touch; but, from his language, manner, and intelligence, I inferred that his color had procured for him the few advantages within the reach of a quick-witted, kindly treated slave. Silent, grave, and thoughtful, but most serviceable, was my contraband; glad of the books I brought him, faithful in the performance of the duties I assigned to him, grateful for the friendliness I could not but feel and show toward him. Often I longed to ask what purpose was so visibly altering his aspect with such daily deepening gloom. But I never dared, and no one else had either time or desire to pry into the past of this specimen of one branch of the chivalrous "F.F.Vs."

On the seventh night, Dr. Franck suggested that it would be well for some one, besides the general watchman of the ward, to be with the captain, as it might be his last. Although the greater part of the two preceding nights had been spent there, of course I offered to remain,—for there is a strange fascination in these scenes, which renders one careless of fatigue and unconscious of fear until the crisis is passed.

"Give him water as long as he can drink, and if he drops into a natural sleep, it may save him. I'll look in at midnight, when some change will probably take place. Nothing but sleep or a miracle will keep him now. Good night."

Away went the Doctor; and, devouring a whole mouthful of grapes, I lowered the lamp, wet the captain's head, and sat down on a hard stool to begin my watch. The captain lay with his hot, haggard face turned toward me, filling the air with his poisonous breath, and feebly muttering, with lips and tongue so parched that the sanest speech would have been difficult to understand. Robert was stretched on his bed in the inner room, the door of which stood ajar, that a fresh draught from his open window might carry the fever-fumes away through mine. I could just see a long, dark figure, with the lighter outline of a face, and, having little else to do just then, I fell to thinking of this curious contraband, who evidently prized his freedom highly, yet seemed in no haste to enjoy it. Doctor Franck had offered to send him on to safer quarters, but he had said, "No, thank yer, Sir, not yet," and then had gone away to fall into one of those black moods of his, which began to disturb me, because I had no power to lighten them. As I sat listening to the clocks from the steeples all about us, I amused myself with planning Robert's future, as I often did my own, and had dealt out to him a generous hand of trumps wherewith to play this game of life which hitherto had gone so cruelly against him, when a harsh, choked voice called, —

"Lucy!"

It was the captain, and some new terror seemed to have gifted him with momentary strength.

"Yes, here's Lucy," I answered, hoping that by following the fancy I might quiet him, — for his face was damp with the clammy moisture, and his frame shaken with the nervous tremor that so often precedes death. His dull eye fixed upon me, dilating with a bewildered look of incredulity and wrath, till he broke out fiercely. —

"That's a lie! she's dead, — and so's Bob, damn him!"

Finding speech a failure, I began to sing the quiet tune that had often soothed delirium like this; but hardly had the line,

"See gentle patience smile on pain,"

passed my lips, when he clutched me by the wrist, whispering like one in mortal fear, —

"Hush! she used to sing that way to Bob, but she never would to me. I swore I'd whip the Devil out of her, and I did; but you know before she cut her throat she said she'd haunt me, and there she is!"

97

He pointed behind me with an aspect of such pale dismay, that I involuntarily glanced over my shoulder and started as if I had seen a veritable ghost; for, peering from the gloom of that inner room, I saw a shadowy face, with dark hair all about it, and a glimpse of scarlet at the throat. An instant showed me that it was only Robert leaning from his bed's-foot, wrapped in a gray army-blanket, with his red shirt just visible above it, and his long hair disordered by sleep. But what a strange expression was on his face! The unmarred side was toward me, fixed and motionless as when I first observed it,—less absorbed now, but more intent. His eye glittered, his lips were apart like one who listened with every sense, and his whole aspect reminded me of a hound to which some wind had brought the scent of unsuspected prey.

"Do you know him, Robert? Does he mean you?"

"Lord, no, Ma'am; they all own half a dozen Bobs: but hearin' my name woke me; that's all."

He spoke quite naturally, and lay down again, while I returned to my charge, thinking that this paroxysm was probably his last. But by another hour I perceived a hopeful change, for the tremor had subsided, the cold dew was gone, his breathing was more regular, and Sleep, the healer, had descended to save or take him gently away. Doctor Franck looked in at midnight, bade me keep all cool and quiet, and not fail to administer a certain draught as soon as the captain woke. Very much relieved, I laid my head on my arms, uncomfortably folded on the little table, and fancied I was about to perform one of the feats which practice renders possible,—"sleeping with one eye open," as we say: a half-and-half doze, for all senses sleep but that of hearing; the faintest murmur, sigh, or motion will break it, and give one back one's wits much brightened by the permission to "stand at ease." On this night, the experiment was a

98

failure, for previous vigils, confinement, and much care had rendered naps a dangerous indulgence, Having roused half a dozen times in an hour to find all quiet, I dropped my heavy head on my arms, and, drowsily resolving to look up again in fifteen minutes, fell fast asleep.

The striking of a deep-voiced clock woke me with a start. "That is one," thought I, but, to my dismay, two more strokes followed; and in remorseful haste I sprang up to see what harm my long oblivion had done. A strong hand put me back into my seat, and held me there. It was Robert. The instant my eye met his my heart began to beat, and all along my nerves tingled that electric flash which foretells a danger that we cannot see. He was very pale, his mouth grim, and both eyes full of sombre fire,—for even the wounded one was open now, all the more sinister for the deep scar above and below. But his touch was steady, his voice quiet, as he said,—

"Sit still, Ma'am; I won't hurt yer, nor even scare yer, if I can help it, but yer waked too soon."

"Let me go, Robert,—the captain is stirring,—I must give him something."

"No, Ma'am, yer can't stir an inch. Look here!"

Holding me with one hand, with the other he took up the glass in which I had left the draught, and showed me it was empty.

"Has he taken it?" I asked, more and more bewildered.

"I flung it out o' winder, Ma'am; he'll have to do without."

"But why, Robert? why did you do it?"

"Because I hate him!"

Impossible to doubt the truth of that; his whole face showed it, as he spoke through his set teeth, and launched a fiery glance at the unconscious captain. I could only hold my breath and stare blankly at him, wondering what mad act was coming next. I suppose I shook and turned white, as women have a foolish habit of doing when sudden danger daunts them; for Robert released my arm, sat down upon the bedside just in front of me, and said, with the ominous quietude that made me cold to see and hear,—

"Don't yer be frightened, Ma'am: don't try to run away, fer the door's locked an' the key in my pocket; don't yer cry out, fer yer'd have to scream a long while, with my hand on yer mouth, before yer was heard. Be still, an' I'll tell yer what I'm goin' to do."

"Lord help us! he has taken the fever in some sudden, violent way, and is out of his head. I must humor him till some one comes"; in pursuance of which swift determination, I tried to say, quite composedly,—

"I will be still and hear you; but open the window. Why did you shut it?"

"I'm sorry I can't do it, Ma'am; but yer'd jump out, or call, if I did, an' I'm not ready yet. I shut it to make yer sleep, an' heat would do it quicker'n anything else I could do."

The captain moved, and feebly muttered, "Water!" Instinctively I rose to give it to him, but the heavy hand came down upon my shoulder, and in the same decided tone Robert said,—=

"The water went with the physic; let him call."

"Do let me go to him! he'll die without care!"

"I mean he shall;—don't yer interfere, if yer please, Ma'am."

In spite of his quiet tone and respectful manner, I saw murder in his eyes, and turned faint with fear; yet the fear excited me, and, hardly knowing what I did, I seized the hands that had seized me, crying,—

"No, no, you shall not kill him! it is base to hurt a helpless man. Why do you hate him? He is not your master?"

"He's my brother."

I felt that answer from head to foot, and seemed to fathom what was coming, with a prescience vague, but unmistakable. One appeal was left to me, and I made it.

"Robert, tell me what it means? Do not commit a crime and make me accessory to it—There is a better way of righting wrong than by violence;—let me help you find it."

My voice trembled as I spoke, and I heard the frightened flutter of my heart; so did he, and if any little act of mine had ever won affection or respect from him, the memory of it served me then. He looked down, and seemed to put some question to himself; whatever it was, the answer was in my favor, for when his eyes rose again, they were gloomy, but not desperate.

"I will tell you, Ma'am; but mind, this makes no difference; the boy is mine. I'll give the Lord a chance to take him fust; if He don't, I shall."

"Oh, no! remember, he is your brother."

An unwise speech; I felt it as it passed my lips, for a black frown gathered on Robert's face, and his strong hands closed with an ugly sort of grip. But he did not touch the poor soul gasping there before

101

him, and seemed content to let the slow suffocation of that stifling room end his frail life.

"I'm not like to forget that, Ma'am, when I've been thinkin' of it all this week. I knew him when they fetched him in, an' would 'a' done it long 'fore this, but I wanted to ask where Lucy was; he knows,— he told to-night,—an' now he's done for."

"Who is Lucy?" I asked hurriedly, intent on keeping his mind busy with any thought but murder.

With one of the swift transitions of a mixed temperament like this, at my question Robert's deep eyes filled, the clenched hands were spread before his face, and all I heard were the broken words,—

"My wife,—he took her—"

In that instant every thought of fear was swallowed up in burning indignation for the wrong, and a perfect passion of pity for the desperate man so tempted to avenge an injury for which there seemed no redress but this. He was no longer slave or contraband, no drop of black blood marred him in my sight, but an infinite compassion yearned to save, to help, to comfort him. Words seemed so powerless I offered none, only put my hand on his poor head, wounded, homeless, bowed down with grief for which I had no cure, and softly smoothed the long neglected hair, pitifully wondering the while where was the wife who must have loved this tender-hearted man so well.

The captain moaned again, and faintly whispered, "Air!" but I never stirred. God forgive me! just then I hated him as only a woman thinking of a sister woman's wrong could hate. Robert looked up; his eyes were dry again, his mouth grim. I saw that, said, "Tell me

102

more," and he did, — for sympathy is a gift the poorest may give, the proudest stoop to receive.

"Yer see, Ma'am, his father, — I might say ours, if I warn't ashamed of both of 'em, — his father died two years ago, an' left us all to Marster Ned, — that's him here, eighteen then. He always hated me, I looked so like old Marster: he don't — only the light skin an' hair. Old Marster was kind to all of us, me 'specially, an' bought Lucy off the next plantation down there in South Car'lina, when he found I liked her. I married her, all I could, Ma'am; it warn't much, but we was true to one another till Marster Ned come home a year after an' made hell fer both of us. He sent my old mother to be used up in his rice swamp in Georgy; he found me with my pretty Lucy, an' though young Miss cried, an' I prayed to him on my knees, an' Lucy run away, he wouldn't have no mercy; he brought her back, an' — took her, Ma'am."

"Oh! what did you do?" I cried, hot with helpless pain and passion.

How the man's outraged heart sent the blood flaming up into his face and deepened the tones of his impetuous voice, as he stretched his arm across the bed, saying, with a terribly expressive gesture, —

"I half murdered him, an' to-night I'll finish."

"Yes, yes, — but go on now; what came next?"

He gave me a look that showed no white man could have felt a deeper degradation in remembering and confessing these last acts of brotherly oppression.

"They whipped me till I couldn't stand, an' then they sold me further South. Yer thought I was a white man once; — look here!"

With a sudden wrench he tore the shirt from neck to waist, and on

103

his strong brown shoulders showed me furrows deeply ploughed, wounds which, though healed, were ghastlier to me than any in that house. I could not speak to him, and, with the pathetic dignity a great grief lends the humblest sufferer, he ended his brief tragedy by simply saying,—

"That's all. Ma'am. I've never seen her since, an' now I never shall in this world,—maybe not in t' other."

"But, Robert, why think her dead? The captain was wandering when he said those sad things; perhaps he will retract them when he is sane. Don't despair; don't give up yet."

"No, Ma'am, I guess he's right; she was too proud to bear that long. It's like her to kill herself. I told her to, if there was no other way; an' she always minded me, Lucy did. My poor girl! Oh, it warn't right! No, by God, it warn't!"

As the memory of this bitter wrong, this double bereavement, burned in his sore heart, the devil that lurks in every strong man's blood leaped up; he put his hand upon his brother's throat, and, watching the white face before him, muttered low between his teeth,—

"I'm lettin' him go too easy; there's no pain in this; we a'n't even yet. I wish he knew me. Marster Ned! it's Bob; where's Lucy?"

From the captain's lips there came a long faint sigh, and nothing but a flutter of the eyelids showed that he still lived. A strange stillness filled the room as the elder brother held the younger's life suspended in his hand, while wavering between a dim hope and a deadly hate. In the whirl of thoughts that went on in my brain, only one was clear enough to act upon. I must prevent murder, if I could,—but how? What could I do up there alone, locked in with a dying man and a lunatic?—for any mind yielded utterly to any unrighteous impulse is mad while the impulse rules it. Strength I had not, nor much courage, neither time nor wit for stratagem, and chance only could bring me help before it was too late. But one weapon I possessed,—a tongue,—often a woman's best defence: and sympathy, stronger than fear, gave me power to use it. What I said Heaven only knows, but surely Heaven helped me; words burned on my lips, tears streamed from my eyes, and some good angel prompted me to use the one name that had power to arrest my hearer's hand and touch his heart. For at that moment I heartily believed that Lucy lived, and this earnest faith roused in him a like belief.

He listened with the lowering look of one in whom brute instinct was sovereign for the time,—a look that makes the noblest countenance base. He was but a man,—a poor, untaught, outcast, outraged man. Life had few joys for him; the world offered him no honors, no success, no home, no love. What future would this crime mar? and why should he deny himself that sweet, yet bitter morsel called revenge? How many white men, with all New England's freedom, culture, Christianity, would not have felt as he felt then? Should I have reproached him for a human anguish, a human longing for redress, all now left him from the ruin of his few poor hopes? Who had taught him that self-control, self-sacrifice, are attributes that make men masters of the earth and lift them nearer heaven? Should I have urged the beauty of forgiveness, the duty of devout submission? He had no religion, for he was no saintly "Uncle Tom," and Slavery's black shadow seemed to darken all the world to him and shut out God. Should I have warned him of penalties, of judgments, and the potency of law? What did he know of justice, or the mercy that should temper that stern virtue, when every law, human and divine, had been broken on his hearthstone?

105

Should I have tried to touch him by appeals to filial duty, to brotherly love? How had his appeals been answered? What memories had father and brother stored up in his heart to plead for either now? No,—all these influences, these associations, would have proved worse than useless, had I been calm enough to try them. I was not; but instinct, subtler than reason, showed me the one safe clue by which to lead this troubled soul from the labyrinth in which it groped and nearly fell. When I paused, breathless, Robert turned to me, asking, as if human assurances could strengthen his faith in Divine Omnipotence,—

"Do you believe, if I let Marster Ned live, the Lord will give me back my Lucy?"

"As surely as there is a Lord, you will find her here or in the beautiful hereafter, where there is no black or white, no master and no slave."

He took his hand from his brother's throat, lifted his eyes from my face to the wintry sky beyond, as if searching for that blessed country, happier even than the happy North. Alas, it was the darkest hour before the dawn!—there was no star above, no light below but the pale glimmer of the lamp that showed the brother who had made him desolate. Like a blind man who believes there is a sun, yet cannot see it, he shook his head, let his arms drop nervously upon his knees, and sat there dumbly asking that question which many a soul whose faith is firmer fixed than his has asked in hours less dark than this,—

"Where is God?" I saw the tide had turned, and strenuously tried to keep this rudderless lifeboat from slipping back into the whirlpool wherein it had been so nearly lost.

"I have listened to you, Robert; now hear me, and heed what I say, because my heart is full of pity for you, full of hope for your future, and a desire to help you now. I want you to go away from here, from the temptation of this place, and the sad thoughts that haunt it. You have conquered yourself once, and I honor you for it, because, the harder the battle, the more glorious the victory; but it is safer to put a greater distance between you and this man. I will write you letters, give you money, and send you to good old Massachusetts to begin your new life a freeman,—yes, and a happy man; for when the captain is himself again, I will learn where Lucy is, and move heaven and earth to find and give her back to you. Will you do this, Robert?"

Slowly, very slowly, the answer came; for the purpose of a week, perhaps a year, was hard to relinquish in an hour.

"Yes, Ma'am, I will."

"Good! Now you are the man I thought you, and I'll work for you with all my heart. You need sleep, my poor fellow; go, and try to forget. The captain is still alive, and as yet you are spared the sin. No, don't look there; I'll care for him. Come, Robert, for Lucy's sake."

Thank Heaven for the immortality of love! for when all other means of salvation failed, a spark of this vital fire softened the man's iron will until a woman's hand could bend it. He let me take from him the key, let me draw him gently away and lead him to the solitude which now was the most healing balm I could bestow. Once in his little room, he fell down on his bed and lay there as if spent with the sharpest conflict of his life. I slipped the bolt across his door, and unlocked my own, flung up the window, steadied myself with a breath of air, then rushed to Doctor Franck. He came; and till dawn we worked together, saving one brother's life, and taking earnest thought how best to secure the other's liberty. When the sun came up as blithely as if it shone only upon happy homes, the Doctor went to Robert. For an hour I heard the murmur of their voices; once I caught the sound of heavy sobs, and for a time a reverent hush, as if in the silence that good man were ministering to soul as well as sense. When he departed he took Robert with him, pausing to tell me he should get him off as soon as possible, but not before we met again.

Nothing more was seen of them all day; another surgeon came to see the captain, and another attendant came to fill the empty place. I tried to rest, but could not, with the thought of poor Lucy tugging at my heart, and was soon back at my post again, anxiously hoping that my contraband had not been too hastily spirited away. Just as night fell there came a tap, and opening, I saw Robert literally "clothed and in his right mind." The Doctor had replaced the ragged suit with tidy garments, and no trace of that tempestuous night remained but deeper lines upon the forehead, and the docile look of a repentant child. He did not cross the threshold, did not offer me his hand,—only took off his cap, saying, with a traitorous falter in his voice,—

"God bless you, Ma'am! I'm goin'."

I put out both my hands, and held his fast.

"Good-bye, Robert! Keep up good heart, and when I come home to Massachusetts we'll meet in a happier place than this. Are you quite ready, quite comfortable for your journey?

"Yes, Ma'am, Yes; the Doctor's fixed everything; I'm goin' with a friend of his; my papers are all right, an' I'm as happy as I can be till I find,—"

He stopped there; then went on, with a glance into the room,—

"I'm glad I didn't do it, an' I thank yer, Ma'am, fer hinderin' me,— thank yer hearty; but I'm afraid I hate him jest the same."

Of course he did; and so did I; for these faulty hearts of ours cannot turn perfect in a night, but need frost and fire, wind and rain, to ripen and make them ready for the great harvest-home. Wishing to divert his mind, I put my poor mite into his hand, and, remembering the magic of a certain little book, I gave him mine, on whose dark cover whitely shone the Virgin Mother and the Child, the grand history of whose life the book contained. The money went into Robert's pocket with a grateful murmur, the book into his bosom with a long took and a tremulous—

"I never saw my baby, Ma'am."

I broke down then; and though my eyes were too dim to see, I felt the touch of lips upon my hands, heard the sound of departing feet, and knew my contraband was gone.

When one feels an intense dislike, the less one says about the subject of it the better; therefore I shall merely record that the captain lived,—in time was exchanged; and that, whoever the other party was, I am convinced the Government got the best of the bargain. But long before this occurred, I had fulfilled my promise to Robert; for as soon as my patient recovered strength of memory enough to make his answer trustworthy, I asked, without any circumlocution,—

"Captain Fairfax, where is Lucy?"

And too feeble to be angry, surprised, or insincere, he straightway answered,—

109

"Dead, Miss Dane."

"And she killed herself, when you sold Bob?"

"How the Devil did you know that?" he muttered, with an expression half-remorseful, half-amazed; but I was satisfied, and said no more.

Of course, this went to Robert, waiting far away there in a lonely home,—waiting, working, hoping for his Lucy. It almost broke my heart to do it; but delay was weak, deceit was wicked; so I sent the heavy tidings, and very soon the answer came,—only three lines; but I felt that the sustaining power of the man's life was gone.

"I thought I'd never see her any more; I'm glad to know she's out of trouble. I thank yer, Ma'am; an' if they let us, I'll fight fer yer till I'm killed, which I hope will be 'fore long."

Six months later he had his wish, and kept his word.

Every one knows the story of the attack on Fort Wagner; but we should not tire yet of recalling how our Fifty-Fourth, spent with three sleepless nights, a day's fast, and a march under the July sun, stormed the fort as night fell, facing death in many shapes, following their brave leaders through a fiery rain of shot and shell, fighting valiantly for God and Governor Andrew,—how the regiment that went into action seven hundred strong came out having had nearly half its number captured, killed, or wounded, leaving their young commander to be buried, like a chief of earlier times, with his body-guard around him, faithful to the death. Surely, the insult turns to honor, and the wide grave needs no monument but the heroism that consecrates it in our sight; surely, the hearts that held him nearest see through their tears a noble victory in the seeming sad defeat; and surely, God's benediction

110

was bestowed, when this loyal soul answered, as Death called the roll, "Lord, here I am, with the brothers Thou hast given me!"

The future must show how well that fight was fought; for though Fort Wagner still defies us, public prejudice is down; and through the cannon smoke of that black night the manhood of the colored race shines before many eyes that would not see, rings in many ears that would not hear, wins many hearts that would not hitherto believe.

When the news came that we were needed, there was none so glad as I to leave teaching contrabands, the new work I had taken up, and go to nurse "our boys," as my dusky flock so proudly called the wounded of the Fifty-Fourth. Feeling more satisfaction, as I assumed my big apron and turned up my cuffs, than if dressing for the President's levee, I fell to work on board the hospital-ship in Hilton-Head harbor. The scene was most familiar, and yet strange; for only dark faces looked up at me from the pallets so thickly laid along the floor, and I missed the sharp accent of my Yankee boys in the slower, softer voices calling cheerily to one another, or answering my questions with a stout, "We'll never give it up, Ma'am, till the last Reb's dead," or, "If our people's free, we can afford to die."

Passing from bed to bed, intent on making one pair of hands do the work of three, at least, I gradually washed, fed, and bandaged my way down the long line of sable heroes, and coming to the very last, found that he was my contraband. So old, so worn, so deathly weak and wan, I never should have known him but for the deep scar on his cheek. That side lay uppermost, and caught my eye at once; but even then I doubted, such an awful change had come upon him, when, turning to the ticket just above his head, I saw the name, "Robert Dane." That both assured and touched me, for, remembering that he had no name, I knew that he had taken mine. I longed for him to speak to me, to tell how he had fared since I lost sight of him, and let me perform some little service for him in return for many he had done for me; but he seemed asleep; and as I stood re-living that strange night again, a bright lad, who lay next him softly waving an old fan across both beds, looked up and said,—

"I guess you know him, Ma'am?"

"You are right. Do you?"

"As much as any one was able to, Ma'am."

"Why do you say 'was,' as if the man were dead and gone?"

"I s'pose because I know he'll have to go. He's got a bad jab in the breast, an' is bleedin' inside, the Doctor says. He don't suffer any, only gets weaker 'n' weaker every minute. I've been fannin' him this long while, an' he's talked a little; but he don't know me now, so he's most gone, I guess."

There was so much sorrow and affection in the boy's face, that I remembered something, and asked, with redoubled interest,—

"Are you the one that brought him off? I was told about a boy who nearly lost his life in saving that of his mate."

I dare say the young fellow blushed, as any modest lad might have done; I could not see it, but I heard the chuckle of satisfaction that escaped him, as he glanced from his shattered arm and bandaged side to the pale figure opposite.

"Lord, Ma'am, that's nothin'; we boys always stan' by one another, an' I warn't goin' to leave him to be tormented any more by them

112

cussed Rebs. He's been a slave once, though he don't look half so much like it as me, an' was born in Boston."

He did not; for the speaker was as black as the ace of spades, — being a sturdy specimen, the knave of clubs would perhaps be a fitter representative, — but the dark freeman looked at the white slave with the pitiful, yet puzzled expression I have so often seen on the faces of our wisest men, when this tangled question of Slavery presents itself, asking to be cut or patiently undone.

"Tell me what you know of this man; for, even if he were awake, he is too weak to talk."

"I never saw him till I joined the regiment, an' no one 'peared to have got much out of him. He was a shut-up sort of feller, an' didn't seem to care for anything but gettin' at the Rebs. Some say he was the fust man of us that enlisted; I know he fretted till we were off, an' when we pitched into old Wagner, he fought like the Devil."

"Were you with him when he was wounded? How was it?"

"Yes, Ma'am. There was somethin' queer about it; for he 'peared to know the chap that killed him, an' the chap knew him. I don't dare to ask, but I rather guess one owned the other some time, — for, when they clinched, the chap sung out, 'Bob!' an' Dane, 'Marster Ned! then they went at it."

I sat down suddenly, for the old anger and compassion struggled in my heart, and I both longed and feared to hear what was to follow.

"You see, when the Colonel — Lord keep an' send him back to us! — it a'n't certain yet, you know, Ma'am, though it's two days ago we lost him — well, when the Colonel shouted, 'Rush on, boys, rush on!' Dane tore away as if he was goin' to take the fort alone; I was next him, an' kept close as we went through the ditch an' up the wall. Hi! warn't that a rusher!" and the boy flung up his well arm with a whoop, as if the mere memory of that stirring moment came over him in a gust of irrepressible excitement.

"Were you afraid?" I said,—asking the question women often put, and receiving the answer they seldom fail to get.

"No, Ma'am!"—emphasis on the "Ma'am,"—"I never thought of anything but the damn Rebs, that scalp, slash, an' cut our ears off, when they git us. I was bound to let daylight into one of 'em at least, an' I did. Hope he liked it!"

"It is evident that you did, and I don't blame you in the least. Now go on about Robert, for I should be at work."

"He was one of the fust up; I was just behind, an' though the whole thing happened in a minute. I remember how it was, for all I was yellin' an' knockin' round like mad. Just where we were, some sort of an officer was wavin' his sword an' cheerin' on his men; Dane saw him by a big flash that come by; he flung away his gun, give a leap, an' went at that feller as if he was Jeff, Beauregard, an' Lee, all in one. I scrabbled after as quick as I could, but was only up in time to see him git the sword straight through him an' drop into the ditch. You needn't ask what I did next, Ma'am, for I don't quite know myself; all I 'm clear about is, that I managed somehow to pitch that Reb into the fort as dead as Moses, git hold of Dane, an' bring him off. Poor old feller! we said we went in to live or die; he said he went in to die, an' he 's done it."

I had been intently watching the excited speaker; but as he regretfully added those last words I turned again, and Robert's eyes met mine,—those melancholy eyes, so full of an intelligence that

114

proved he had heard, remembered, and reflected with that preternatural power which often outlives all other faculties. He knew me, yet gave no greeting; was glad to see a woman's face, yet had no smile wherewith to welcome it; felt that he was dying, yet uttered no farewell. He was too far across the river to return or linger now; departing thought, strength, breath, were spent in one grateful look, one murmur of submission to the last pang he could ever feel. His lips moved, and, bending to them, a whisper chilled my cheek, as it shaped the broken words, —

"I would have done it, — but it 's better so, — I'm satisfied."

Ah! well he might be, — for, as he turned his face from the shadow of the life that was, the sunshine of the life to be touched it with a beautiful content, and in the drawing of a breath my contraband found wife and home, eternal liberty and God.

Nelly sat beside her mother picking lint; but while her fingers flew, her eyes often looked wistfully out into the meadow, golden with buttercups, and bright with sunshine. Presently she said, rather bashfully, but very earnestly, "Mamma, I want to tell you a little plan I've made, if you'll please not laugh."

"I think I can safely promise that, my dear," said her mother, putting down her work that she might listen quite respectfully.

Nelly looked pleased, and went on confidingly,

"Since brother Will came home with his lame foot, and I've helped you tend him, I've heard a great deal about hospitals, and liked it very much. To-day I said I wanted to go and be a nurse, like Aunt Mercy; but Will laughed, and told me I'd better begin by nursing sick birds and butterflies and pussies before I tried to take care of men. I did not like to be made fun of, but I've been thinking that it would be very pleasant to have a little hospital all my own, and be a nurse in it, because, if I took pains, so many pretty creatures might be made well, perhaps. Could I, mamma?"

Her mother wanted to smile at the idea, but did not, for Nelly looked up with her heart and eyes so full of tender compassion, both for the unknown men for whom her little hands had done their best, and for the smaller sufferers nearer home, that she stroked the shining head, and answered readily: "Yes, Nelly, it will be a proper charity for such a young Samaritan, and you may learn much if you are in earnest. You must study how to feed and nurse your little patients, else your pity will do no good, and your hospital become a prison. I will help you, and Tony shall be your surgeon."

"O mamma, how good you always are to me! Indeed, I am in truly earnest; I will learn, I will be kind, and may I go now and begin?"

"You may, but tell me first where will you have your hospital?"

"In my room, mamma; it is so snug and sunny, and I never should forget it there," said Nelly.

"You must not forget it anywhere. I think that plan will not do. How would you like to find caterpillars walking in your bed, to hear sick pussies mewing in the night, to have beetles clinging to your clothes, or see mice, bugs, and birds tumbling downstairs whenever the door was open?" said her mother.

Nelly laughed at that thought a minute, then clapped her hands, and cried: "Let us have the old summer-house! My doves only use the upper part, and it would be so like Frank in the storybook. Please say yes again, mamma."

Her mother did say yes, and, snatching up her hat, Nelly ran to find Tony, the gardener's son, a pleasant lad of twelve, who was Nelly's favorite playmate. Tony pronounced the plan a "jolly" one, and, leaving his work, followed his young mistress to the summer-house, for she could not wait one minute.

"What must we do first?" she asked, as they stood looking in at the dusty room, full of garden tools, bags of seeds, old flower-pots, and watering-cans.

"Clear out the rubbish, miss," answered Tony.

"Here it goes, then," and Nelly began bundling everything out in such haste that she broke two flower-pots, scattered all the squash-seeds, and brought a pile of rakes and hoes clattering down about her ears.

"Just wait a bit, and let me take the lead, miss. You hand me things, I'll pile 'em in the barrow and wheel 'em off to the barn; then it will save time, and be finished up tidy."

Nelly did as he advised, and very soon nothing but dust remained.

"What next?" she asked, not knowing in the least.

"I'll sweep up while you see if Polly can come and scrub the room out. It ought to be done before you stay here, let alone the patients."

"So it had," said Nelly, looking very wise all of a sudden. "Will says the wards—that means the rooms, Tony—are scrubbed every day or two, and kept very clean, and well venti-something—I can't say it; but it means having a plenty of air come in. I can clean windows while Polly mops, and then we shall soon be done." Away she ran, feeling very busy and important. Polly came, and very soon the room looked like another place. The four latticed windows were set wide open, so the sunshine came dancing through the vines that grew outside, and curious roses peeped in to see what frolic was afoot. The walls shone white again, for not a spider dared to stay; the wide seat which encircled the room was dustless now,—the floor as nice as willing hands could make it; and the south wind blew away all musty odors with its fragrant breath.

"How fine it looks!" cried Nelly, dancing on the doorstep, lest a foot-print should mar the still damp floor.

"I'd almost like to fall sick for the sake of staying here," said Tony, admiringly. "Now, what sort of beds are you going to have, miss?

"I suppose it won't do to put butterflies and toads and worms into beds like the real soldiers where Will was?" answered Nelly, looking anxious.

Tony could hardly help shouting at the idea; but, rather than trouble his little mistress, he said very soberly: "I'm afraid they wouldn't lay easy, not being used to it. Tucking up a butterfly would about kill him; the worms would be apt to get lost among the bed-clothes; and the toads would tumble out the first thing."

"I shall have to ask mamma about it. What will you do while I'm gone?" said Nelly, unwilling that a moment should be lost.

"I'll make frames for nettings to the windows, else the doves will come in and eat up the sick people.

"I think they will know that it is a hospital, and be too kind to hurt or frighten their neighbors," began Nelly; but as she spoke, a plump white dove walked in, looked about with its red-ringed eyes, and quietly pecked up a tiny bug that had just ventured out from the crack where it had taken refuge when the deluge came.

"Yes, we must have the nettings. I'll ask mamma for some lace," said Nelly, when she saw that; and, taking her pet dove on her shoulder, told it about her hospital as she went toward the house; for, loving all little creatures as she did, it grieved her to have any harm befall even the least or plainest of them. She had a sweet child-fancy that her playmates understood her language as she did theirs, and that birds, flowers, animals, and insects felt for her the same affection which she felt for them. Love always makes friends, and nothing seemed to fear the gentle child; but welcomed her like a little sun who shone alike on all, and never suffered an eclipse.

She was gone some time, and when she came back her mind was

full of new plans, one hand full of rushes, the other of books, while over her head floated the lace, and a bright green ribbon hung across her arm.

"Mamma says that the best beds will be little baskets, boxes, cages, and any sort of thing that suits the patients; for each will need different care and food and medicine. I have not baskets enough, so, as I cannot have pretty white beds, I am going to braid pretty green nests for my patients, and, while I do it, mamma thought you'd read to me the pages she has marked, so that we may begin right."

"Yes, miss; I like that. But what is the ribbon for?" asked Tony.

"O, that's for you. Will says that, if you are to be an army surgeon, you must have a green band on your arm; so I got this to tie on when we play hospital."

Tony let her decorate the sleeve of his gray jacket, and when the nettings were done, the welcome books were opened and enjoyed. It was a happy time, sitting in the sunshine, with leaves pleasantly astir all about them, doves cooing overhead, and flowers sweetly gossiping together through the summer afternoon. Nelly wove her smooth, green rushes. Tony pored over his pages, and both found something better than fairy legends in the family histories of insects, birds, and beasts. All manner of wonders appeared, and were explained to them, till Nelly felt as if a new world had been given her, so full of beauty, interest, and pleasure that she never could be tired of studying it. Many of these things were not strange to Tony, because, born among plants, he had grown up with them as if they were brothers and sisters, and the sturdy, brown-faced boy had learned many lessons which no poet or philosopher could have taught him, unless he had become as child-like a s himself, and studied from the same great book.

When the baskets were done, the marked pages all read, and the sun began to draw his rosy curtains round him before smiling "Good night," Nelly ranged the green beds round the room, Tony put in the screens, and the hospital was ready. The little nurse was so excited that she could hardly eat her supper, and directly afterwards ran up to tell Will how well she had succeeded with the first part of her enterprise. Now brother Will was a brave young officer, who had fought stoutly and done his duty like a man. But when lying weak and wounded at home, the cheerful courage which had led him safely through many dangers seemed to have deserted him, and he was often gloomy, sad, or fretful, because he longed to be at his post again, and time passed very slowly. This troubled his mother, and made Nelly wonder why he found lying in a pleasant room so much harder than fighting battles or making weary marches. Anything that interested and amused him was very welcome, and when Nelly, climbing on the arm of his sofa, told her plans, mishaps, and successes, he laughed out more heartily than he had done for many a day, and his thin face began to twinkle with fun as it used to do so long ago. That pleased Nelly, and she chatted like any affectionate little magpie, till Will was really interested; for when one is ill, small things amuse.

"Do you expect your patients to come to you, Nelly?" he asked.

"No, I shall go and look for them. I often see poor things suffering in the garden, and the wood, and always feel as if they ought to be taken care of, as people are."

"You won't like to carry insane bugs, lame toads, and convulsive kittens in your hands, and they would not stay on a stretcher if you had one. You should have an ambulance and be a branch of the Sanitary Commission," said Will.

Nelly had often heard the words, but did not quite understand what they meant. So Will told her of that great never-failing charity, to which thousands owe their lives; and the child listened with lips apart, eyes often full, and so much love and admiration in her heart that she could find no words in which to tell it. When her brother paused, she said earnestly: "Yes, I will be a Sanitary. This little cart of mine shall be my amb'lance, and I'll never let my water-barrels go empty, never drive too fast, or be rough with my poor passengers, like some of the men you tell about. Does this look like an ambulance, Will?"

"Not a bit, but it shall, if you and mamma like to help me. I want four long bits of cane, a square of white cloth, some pieces of thin wood, and the gum-pot," said Will, sitting up to examine the little cart, feeling like a boy again as he took out his knife and began to whittle. Upstairs and downstairs ran Nelly till all necessary materials were collected, and almost breathlessly she watched her brother arch the canes over the cart, cover them with the cloth, and fit an upper shelf of small compartments, each lined with cotton-wool to serve as beds for wounded insects, lest they should hurt one another or jostle out. The lower part was left free for any larger creatures which Nelly might find. Among her toys she had a tiny cask which only needed a peg to be water-tight; this was filled and fitted in before, because, as the small sufferers needed no seats, there was no place for it behind, and, as Nelly was both horse and driver, it was more convenient in front. On each side of it stood a box of stores. In one were minute rollers, as bandages are called, a few bottles not yet filled, and a wee doll's jar of cold-cream, because Nelly could not feel that her outfit was complete without a medicine-chest. The other box was full of crumbs, bits of sugar, bird-seed, and grains of wheat and corn, lest any famished stranger should die for want of food before she got it home. Then mamma painted "U.S. San. Com." in bright letters on the cover, and Nelly received her charitable plaything with a long sigh of satisfaction.

"Nine o'clock already. Bless me, what a short evening this has been," exclaimed Will, as Nelly came to give him her good-night kiss.

"And such a happy one," she answered.

"Thank you very, very much, dear Will. I only wish my little amb'lance was big enough for you to go in,—I'd so like to give you the first ride."

"Nothing I should like better, if it were possible, though I've a prejudice against ambulances in general. But as I cannot ride, I'll try and hop out to your hospital to-morrow, and see how you get on,"—which was a great deal for Captain Will to say, because he had been too listless to leave his sofa for several days.

That promise sent Nelly happily away to bed, only stopping to pop her head out of the window to see if it was likely to be a fair day to-morrow, and to tell Tony about the new plan as he passed below.

"Where shall you go to look for your first load of sick folks, miss?" he asked.

"All round the garden first, then through the grove, and home across the brook. Do you think I can find any patients so?" said Nelly.

"I know you will. Good night, miss," and Tony walked away with a merry look on his face, that Nelly would not have understood if she had seen it.

Up rose the sun bright and early, and up rose Nurse Nelly almost

123

as early and as bright. Breakfast was taken in a great hurry, and before the dew was off the grass this branch of the S. C. was all astir. Papa, mamma, big brother and baby sister, men and maids, all looked out to see the funny little ambulance depart, and nowhere in all the summer fields was there a happier child than Nelly, as she went smiling down the garden path, where tall flowers kissed her as she passed and every blithe bird seemed singing a "Good speed!"

"How I wonder what I shall find first," she thought, looking sharply on all sides as she went. Crickets chirped, grasshoppers leaped, ants worked busily at their subterranean houses, spiders spun shining webs from twig to twig, bees were coming for their bags of gold, and butterflies had just begun their holiday. A large white one alighted on the top of the ambulance, walked over the inscription as if spelling it letter by letter, then floated away from flower to flower, like one carrying the good news far and wide.

"Now every one will know about the hospital and be glad to see me coming," thought Nelly. And indeed it seemed so, for just then a black-bird, sitting on a garden wall, burst out with a song full of musical joy, Nelly's kitten came running after to stare at the wagon and rub her soft side against it, a bright-eyed toad looked out from his cool bower among the lily-leaves, and at that minute Nelly found her first patient. In one of the dewy cobwebs hanging from a shrub near by sat a fat black and yellow spider, watching a fly whose delicate wings were just caught in the net. The poor fly buzzed pitifully, and struggled so hard that the whole web shook: but the more he struggled, the more he entangled himself, and the fierce spider was preparing to descend that it might weave a shroud about its prey, when a little finger broke the threads and lifted the fly safely into the palm of a hand, where he lay faintly humming his thanks.

124

Nelly had heard much about contrabands, knew who they were, and was very much interested in them; so, when she freed the poor black fly she played he was her contraband, and felt glad that her first patient was one that needed help so much. Carefully brushing away as much of the web as she could, she left small Pompey, as she named him, to free his own legs, lest her clumsy fingers should hurt him; then she laid him in one of the soft beds with a grain or two of sugar if he needed refreshment, and bade him rest and recover from his fright, remembering that he was at liberty to fly away whenever he liked, because she had no wish to male a slave of him.

Feeling very happy over this new friend, Nelly went on singing softly as she walked, and presently she found a pretty caterpillar dressed in brown fur, although the day was warm. He lay so still she thought him dead, till he rolled himself into a ball as she touched him.

"I think you are either faint from the heat of this thick coat of yours, or that you are going to make a cocoon of yourself, Mr. Fuzz," said Nelly.

"Now I want to see you turn into a butterfly, so I shall take you, and if get lively again I will let you go. I shall play that you have given out on a march, as the soldiers sometimes do, and been left behind for the Sanitary people to see to."

In went sulky Mr. Fuzz, and on trundled the ambulance till a golden green rose-beetle was discovered, lying on his back kicking as if in a fit.

"Dear me, what shall I do for him?" thought Nelly. "He acts as baby did when she was so ill, and mamma put her in a warm bath. I

125

haven't got my little tub here, or any hot water, and I'm afraid the beetle would not like it if I had. Perhaps he has pain in his stomach; I'll turn him over, and pat his back, as nurse does baby's when she cries for pain like that."

She set the beetle on his legs, and did her best to comfort him; but he was evidently in great distress, for he could not walk, and instead of lifting his emerald overcoat, and spreading the wings that lay underneath, be turned over again, and kicked more violently than before. Not knowing what to do, Nelly put him into one of her soft nests for Tony to cure if possible. She found no more patients in the garden except a dead bee, which she wrapped in a leaf, and took home to bury. When she came to the grove, it was so green and cool she longed to sit and listen to the whisper of the pines, and watch the larch-tassels wave in the wind. But, recollecting her charitable errand, she went rustling along the pleasant path till she came to another patient, over which she stood considering several minutes before she could decide whether it was best to take it to her hospital, because it was a little gray snake, with bruised tail. She knew it would not hurt her, yet she was afraid of it; she thought it pretty, yet could not like it: she pitied its pain, yet shrunk from helping it, for it had a fiery eye, and a keep quivering tongue, that looked as if longing to bite.

"He is a rebel, I wonder if I ought to be good to him," thought Nelly, watching the reptile writhe with pain. "Will said there were sick rebels in his hospital, and one was very kind to him. It says, too, in my little book, 'Love your enemies.' I think snakes are mine, but I guess I'll try and love him because God made him. Some boy will kill him if I leave him here, and then perhaps his mother will be very sad about it. Come, poor worm, I wish to help you, so be patient, and don't frighten me."

Then Nelly laid her little handkerchief on the ground, and with a stick gently lifted the wounded snake upon it, and, folding it together, laid it in the ambulance. She was thoughtful after that, and so busy puzzling her young head about the duty of loving those who hate us, and being kind to those who are disagreeable or unkind, that she went through the rest of the wood quite forgetful of her work. A soft "Queek, queek!" made her look up and listen. The sound came from the long meadow-grass, and, bending it carefully back, she found a half-fledged bird, with one wing trailing on the ground, and its eyes dim with pain or hunger.

"You darling thing, did you fall out of your nest and hurt your wing?" cried Nelly, looking up into the single tree that stood near by. No nest was to be seen, no parent birds hovered overhead, and little Robin could only tell its troubles in that mournful "Queek, queek, queek!"

Nelly ran to get both her chests, and, sitting down beside the bird, tried to feed it. To her joy it ate crumb after crumb, as if it were half starved, and soon fluttered nearer a confiding fearlessness that made her very proud. Soon baby Robin seemed quite comfortable, his eye brightened, he "queeked" no more, and but for the drooping wing would have been himself again. With one of her bandages Nelly bound both wings closely to his sides for fear he should hurt himself by trying to fly; and though he seemed amazed at her proceedings, he behaved very well, only staring at her, and ruffling up his few feathers in a funny way that made her laugh. Then she had to discover some way of accommodating her two larger patients so that neither should hurt nor alarm the other. A bright thought came to her after much pondering. Carefully lifting the handkerchief, she pinned the two ends to the roof of the cart, and there swung little Forked-tongue, while Rob lay easily below.

By this time, Nelly began to wonder how it happened that she found so many more injured things than ever before. But it never entered her innocent head that Tony had searched the wood and meadow before she was up, and laid most of these creatures ready to her hands, that she might not be disappointed. She had not yet lost her faith in fairies, so she fancied they too belonged to her small sisterhood, and presently it did really seem impossible to doubt that the good folk had been at work.

Coming to the bridge that crossed the brook, she stopped a moment to watch the water ripple over the bright pebbles, the ferns bend down to drink, and the funny tadpoles frolic in quieter nooks, where the sun shone, and the dragon-flies swung among the rushes. When Nelly turned to go on, her blue eyes opened wide, and the handle of the ambulance dropped with a noise that caused a stout frog to skip into the water heels over head. Directly in the middle of the bridge was a pretty green tent, made of two tall burdock leaves. The stems were stuck into cracks between the boards, the tips were pinned together with a thorn, and one great buttercup nodded in the doorway like a sleepy sentinel. Nelly stared and smiled, listened, and looked about on every side. Nothing was seen but the quiet meadow and the shady grove, nothing was heard but the babble of the brook and the cheery music of the bobolinks.

"Yes," said Nelly softly to herself, "that is a fairy tent, and in it I may find a baby elf sick with whooping-cough or scarlet-fever. How splendid it would be! only I could never nurse such a dainty thing."

Stooping eagerly, she peeped over the buttercup's drowsy head, and saw what seemed a tiny cock of hay. She had no time to feel disappointed, for the haycock began to stir, and, looking nearer, she beheld two silvery gray mites, who wagged wee tails, and stretched themselves as if they had just waked up. Nelly knew that they were young field-mice, and rejoiced over them, feeling rather relieved that no fairy had appeared, though she still believed them to have had a hand in the matter.

"I shall call the mice my Babes in the Wood, because they are lost and covered up with leaves," said Nelly, as she laid them in her snuggest bed, where they nestled close together, and fell fast asleep again.

Being very anxious to get home, that she might tell her adventures, and show how great was the need of a sanitary commission in that region, Nelly marched proudly up the avenue, and, having displayed her load, hurried to the hospital, where another applicant was waiting for her. On the step of the door lay a large turtle, with one claw gone, and on his back was pasted a bit of paper, with his name,—"Commodore Waddle, U.S.N." Nelly knew this was a joke of Will's, but welcomed the ancient mariner, and called Tony to help her get him in.

All that morning they were very busy settling the new-comers, for both people and books had to be consulted before they could decide what diet and treatment was best for each. The winged contraband had taken Nelly at her word, and flown away on the journey home. Little Rob was put in a large cage, where he could use his legs, yet not injure his lame wing. Forked-tongue lay under a wire cover, on sprigs of fennel, for the gardener said that snakes were fond of it. The Babes in the Wood were put to bed in one of the rush baskets, under a cotton-wool coverlet. Greenback, the beetle, found ease for his unknown aches in the warm heart of a rose, where he sunned himself all day. The Commodore was made happy in a tub of water, grass, and stones, and Mr. Fuzz was put in a well-ventilated glass box to decide whether he would be a cocoon or not.

Tony had not been idle while his mistress was away, and he showed her the hospital garden he had made close by, in which were cabbage, nettle, and mignonette plants for the butterflies, flowering herbs for the bees, chick-weed and hemp for the birds, catnip for the pussies, and plenty of room left for whatever other patients might need. In the afternoon, while Nelly did her task at lint-picking, talking busily to Will as she worked, and interesting him in her affairs, Tony cleared a pretty spot in the grove for the burying-ground, and made ready some small bits of slate on which to write the names of those who died. He did not have it ready an hour too soon, for at sunset two little graves were needed, and Nurse Nelly shed tender tears for her first losses as she laid the motherless mice in one smooth hollow, and the gray-coated rebel in the other. She had learned to care for him already, and when she found him dead, was very glad she had been kind to him, hoping that he knew it, and died happier in her hospital than all alone in the shadowy wood.

The rest of Nelly's patients prospered, and of the many added afterward few died, because of Tony's skilful treatment and her own faithful care. Every morning when the day proved fair the little ambulance went out upon its charitable errand; every afternoon Nelly worked for the human sufferers whom she loved; and every evening brother Will read aloud to her from useful books, showed her wonders with his microscope, or prescribed remedies for the patients, whom he soon knew by name and took much interest in. It was Nelly's holiday; but, though she studied no lessons, she learned much, and unconsciously made her pretty play both an example and a rebuke for others.

At first it seemed a childish pastime, and people laughed. But there was something in the familiar words "sanitary," "hospital" and "ambulance" that made them pleasant sounds to many ears. As reports of Nelly's work went through the neighborhood, other children came to see and copy her design. Rough lads looked ashamed when in her wards they found harmless creatures hurt by them, and going out they said among themselves, "We won't stone birds, chase butterflies, and drown the girls' little cats any more, though we won't tell them so." And most of the lads kept their word so well that people said there never had been so many birds before as all that summer haunted wood and field. Tender-hearted playmates brought their pets to be cured; even busy farmers bad a friendly word for the small charity, which reminded them so sweetly of the great one which should never be forgotten; lonely mothers sometimes looked out with wet eyes as the little ambulance went by, recalling thoughts or absent sons who might be journeying painfully to some far-off hospital, where brave women waited to tend them with hands as willing, hearts as tender, as those the gentle child gave to her self-appointed task.

At home the charm worked also. No more idle days for Nelly, or fretful ones for Will, because the little sister would not neglect the helpless creatures so dependent upon her, and the big brother was ashamed to complain after watching the patience of these lesser sufferers, and merrily said he would try to bear his own wound as quietly and bravely as the "Commodore" bore his. Nelly never knew how much good she had done Captain Will till he went away again in the early autumn. Then he thanked her for it, and though she cried for joy and sorrow she never forgot it, because he left something behind him which always pleasantly reminded her of the double success her little hospital had won.

131

When Will was gone and she had prayed softly in her heart that God would keep him safe and bring him home again, she dried her tears and went away to find comfort in the place where he had spent so many happy hours with her. She had not been there before that day, and when she reached the door she stood quite still and wanted very much to cry again, far something beautiful had happened. She had often asked Will for a motto for her hospital, and he had promised to find her one. She thought he had forgotten it; but even in the hurry of that busy day he had found time to do more than keep his word, while Nelly sat indoors, lovingly brightening the tarnished buttons on the blue coat that had seen so many battles.

Above the roof, where the doves cooed in the sun, now rustled a white flag with the golden "S.C." shining on it as the wind tossed it to and fro. Below, on the smooth panel of the door, a skilful pencil had drawn two arching ferns, in whose soft shadow, poised upon a mushroom, stood a little figure of Nurse Nelly, and underneath it another of Dr. Tony bottling medicine, with spectacles upon his nose. Both hands of the miniature Nelly were outstretched, as if beckoning to a train of insects, birds and beasts, which was so long that it not only circled round the lower rim of this fine sketch, but dwindled in the distance to mere dots and lines. Such merry conceits as one found there! A mouse bringing the tail it had lost in some cruel trap, a dor-bug with a shade over its eyes, an invalid butterfly carried in a tiny litter by long-legged spiders, a fat frog with gouty feet hopping upon crutches, Jenny Wren sobbing in a nice handkerchief, as she brought dear dead Cock Robin to be restored to life. Rabbits, lambs, cats, calves, and turtles, all came trooping up to be healed by the benevolent little maid who welcomed them so heartily.

132

Nelly laughed at these comical mites till the tears ran down her cheeks, and thought she never could be tired of looking at them. But presently she saw four lines clearly printed underneath her picture, and her childish face grew sweetly serious as she read the words of a great poet, which Will had made both compliment and motto: —

> "He prayeth best who loveth best
> All things, both great and small;
> For the dear God who loveth us,
> He made and loveth all."

www.ingramcontent.com/pod-product-compliance
Lightning Source LLC
Chambersburg PA
CBHW011514170626
46810CB00009B/3363